MW00437348

FOUR WARNED

Teas & Temptations Mysteries
Book Four

CINDY STARK

www.cindystark.com

Four Warned © 2018 C. Nielsen

Cover Design by Kelli Ann Morgan
Inspire Creative Services

License Notes

Welcome to Stonebridge, Massachusetts

Welcome to Stonebridge, a small town in Massachusetts where the label "witch" is just as dangerous now as it was in 1692. From a distance, most would say the folks in Stonebridge are about the friendliest around. But a dark and disturbing history is the backbone that continues to haunt citizens of this quaint town where many have secrets they never intend to reveal.

Visit www.cindystark.com for more titles and release information. Sign up for Cindy's newsletter to ensure you're always hearing the latest happenings.

PROLOGUE

Stonebridge, Massachusetts 1689

Clarabelle walked swiftly and surely through the pre-dusk light. An eerie wind blew through the trees, causing the growing shadows to lurk like predators. She constantly searched left and right for anyone who might see her sneak away.

She, Eliza, and Lily wouldn't have long before they were missed. If their fathers discovered where they had gone and their intentions, they likely wouldn't live long enough to fear persecution by the townsfolk.

Genevieve and her mother had been sentenced to death nearly a month ago, but many in town still lived on the edge of paranoia, searching for the next person to condemn as a witch. Clarabelle had been warned not to do anything that would cast doubt about her belief in the righteous leaders of the church.

She narrowed her gaze as a fresh wave of painful sorrow overwhelmed her heart over the loss of a dear friend and sister witch. No, she would not do anything in the open where villagers could see, but she also would not let Genevieve's death go unanswered.

When she neared their meeting grounds, deep in the old grove, she slipped behind a tree and waited. The whispering winds made it hard to listen for anyone who might be nearby, and she didn't want to venture further without ensuring she was alone.

She closed her eyes and whispered. "The song is over, dear winds. The dance is at an end. Pause for a moment to take a rest, before the loving maestro lifts her bow to start again. Bring quiet to the forest, I ask of thee. A hush to nature, so mote it be."

The stiff breeze died so quickly that she worried she might have forced all oxygen from the atmosphere. She filled her lungs to reassure herself and then relaxed. With her eyes still closed, she listened and reached out with other senses searching for anything that didn't belong.

A minute drifted by, but...nothing.

She smiled and nodded to herself before continuing on her way.

When Clarabelle arrived at the circle, she wasn't happy to discover Genevieve's sister, Scarlet, sitting in the grass next to Lily with their heads bent together. Wood had been gathered and laid before them in preparation for a fire.

They both looked up with guilty expressions.

Lily held out a hand toward Clarabelle. "So glad you made it here safely, dear sister."

Clarabelle nodded in greeting, took her hand, and squeezed. "Same to you, sister."

She turned her gaze to Scarlet and sat, forming more of the circle. Even though Scarlet was two years younger than the rest of them, she looked so much like Genevieve with her curly red hair and fire blazing in her green eyes. "Why are you here? Isn't it enough that your family has lost two loved ones? You shouldn't endanger yourself like this, not when we can handle matters for you."

A strong defiance reared inside Genevieve's younger sister and emanated outward. "Of all of you, I have the most right to be here. I am the one who lost the most."

Clarabelle slid an unhappy gaze toward Lily who twisted a dark braid around her finger instead of meeting Clarabelle's gaze. She'd obviously been the one to disclose their intended meeting to Scarlet. "That is true. But, what about your father? He needs you."

Fury spit sparks from Scarlet's eyes. "My father is a shell of the man he once was. These people destroyed him. He might as well be dead, too."

Anguish tore at Clarabelle's heart, further stirring her anger. None in Genevieve's family had deserved to be tortured and destroyed. She and her sisters *would* avenge their deaths.

She gave Scarlet an acknowledging nod. "I understand. Our powers will be stronger with you taking your sister's place, but you must promise the utmost care. Protect yourself at all costs. We all owe that to Genevieve."

Scarlet gave her a cold smile. "Do not fear, sister. I no longer possess the same fears as my mother and Genevieve did. I am not afraid to learn no matter how dark or bloody the spells you intend. I have already lost everything. To take my life now would be a blessing, but I shall make them pay first."

"Yes," hissed Lily. "They shall pay for their ignorance and cruelty."

Clarabelle couldn't argue that. Fiery vengeance burned deep within her soul, and she intended to release it upon those who'd persecuted her friend.

Eliza arrived last, her long blond hair tangled about her shoulders and her breaths deep. She sank to the grass and completed the circle. "Sorry. I had to sneak away, and my mother wouldn't let me out of her sight until all the evening chores were done."

Clarabelle glanced at the small group of fierce women. "Heretofore, we will only meet on a new moon, and only then if we deem it safe. If we are to succeed, we must stay hidden until we can learn to conjure powers that no man can undermine."

The other three witches murmured their agreement.

She thought of dear Genevieve the last time they'd sat in this circle together, and tears sprang to her eyes. "They cannot make us leave this town. It belongs to us, too."

Eliza nodded. "My family was one of the first to settle this area. We've been here longer than most."

Lily threw a twig onto the pile of leaves, sticks and small pieces of wood. "We need to show them that they can't control us. I say we craft a curse that prevents them from ever making us leave."

Clarabelle liked that idea. "A curse that ensures someone in our line will always reside in Stonebridge, that they will never erase us. They did not allow our poor Genevieve to live long enough to bear a child, but her line shall be carried on through her sister." She glanced to Scarlet, hoping that would give her some comfort.

Scarlet scanned the faces of the rest of them, her eyes intense. "That's not enough," she demanded. "I want a life for a life."

A sinister look hovered in the shadow of Lily's eyes. "Yes. They deserve to pay, and no matter how many years pass, they will not be able to forget what they've done. A life now, and another every year on the same date."

Eliza shook her head. Powerful fear filled her gaze and left her body stiff. "No. That's too much. We don't have that kind of power, and it will be dangerous for us to attempt that spell."

Clarabelle sensed Scarlet's and Lily's anger taking a turn toward frenzy. She wanted to make the town suffer for its cruelty, too, but they couldn't afford to be reckless. "What do you suggest, Eliza?"

Eliza studied the unlit fire for several long moments and then looked up. "One person every forty years, and that person shall die on May Day."

"That's too long," Scarlet complained. "I might not be around to witness the next one."

Lily scoffed. "We might not be around to witness the next solstice."

Eliza held up a hand to halt the conversation. "Forty years is long enough that no one will be able to forget. We will ensure others pass down the lore through future generations. It's also a spell that we can reasonably create. We want this to work, don't we?"

Clarabelle nodded. "She is right. Forty years on May Day. When the death occurs, no one will be able to deny the great pain we endured and the retribution that followed."

The wind kicked up, whistling through the tall trees overhead, and teased their hair. Scarlet glanced to Lily who held her gaze for several seconds, and then they both nodded. Clarabelle wasn't sure how, but she sensed that they'd communicated on a deeper level. She would be careful to remember that.

Lily slipped a small book from the waist of her skirt. "I was able to find my family's ancient spell book that my mother had hidden away."

Her declaration caught Clarabelle by surprise. "How?" She and Lily had been certain that her mother had hidden it behind powerful magic.

Lily shrugged. "I prayed to the Blessed Mother to give me access to what was mine, and then I opened my senses and followed my instincts. It was in a place I'd already looked."

Eliza widened her eyes. "Don't let your mother find out."

A crafty smile curved Lily's lips. "She won't. I've hidden its absence behind another spell. She would only discover it missing if she physically tried to pick it up. Which she won't. She's too afraid."

But Lily wasn't afraid. Clarabelle both admired her for that and fretted over it.

Lily opened the book while the rest stared in awe of its ancient power. She thumbed through pages and then glanced up, meeting each of their gazes. "We will need representation of the four elements. My air is obviously present in the wind. Clarabelle, you will need to keep one hand in contact with the earth while we cast the spell. Scarlet will light the fire when we are ready to begin."

Lily paused to reach into her sleeve, and she produced a small bottle. "Lastly, I've brought water for Eliza."

Excitement and anxiety thrummed through Clarabelle's veins. They were really going to do this.

Eliza wrapped her arms about her waist. "How do we know which words to say?"

Lily shook her head. "You won't speak. Only I will since I'll be using the ancient language, and none of you are versed in it."

"Are you?" Clarabelle asked. As much as she wanted to complete the spells, she needed to be sure they could.

Lily's eyes brightened. "I have been burning candles late into the night so that I might study. The words have come easy to me, which can only mean I was meant to learn them. If we are ever able to congregate for long periods of time, I will teach you, too."

The group seemed to accept that.

Lily turned the book to show them. "By altering a few words in this one, I believe it will work for us." She glanced at Scarlet. "Did you bring the knife?"

She nodded and handed the short, bejeweled dagger to Lily. None of them needed to ask if this kind of spell would require blood.

"Are we ready then?" Lily asked, waiting for a nod from each before she shifted her gaze to the next witch.

When all had agreed, Lily drew the knife across her palm, leaving a red trail in its wake. "I will hold my blood up to the wind. Eliza, drop yours into the water, and Clarabelle, press yours into the earth. When we have all done ours, then Scarlet, you will light the fire. We will need a drop of your blood to fall into the flames to start the ritual and then end it."

She passed the knife to Eliza who winced as she cut her flesh and then passed it on.

Clarabelle wrapped her fingers around the hilt and gasped as powerful energy flooded her. She could only imagine what Scarlet would feel when her blood joined the others.

She slid the sharp edge of the knife across her palm and allowed vengeful hatred to infiltrate every part of her body and soul. Power sizzled inside, and she inhaled deeply, soaking up the heady feeling.

She handed the knife to Scarlet with a smile. Her new sister returned the gesture and nodded.

Yes. Together, they would become a force that no one could stop.

"Light the fire, Scarlet," Lily said. "The rest of you make ready. We won't have long once it's burning."

Scarlet inhaled a deep breath and focused on the logs. Thin tendrils of smoke curled upward. A tiny flame burst in the dried grass and immediately spread to the twigs. The small flame grew larger, and the pieces of wood popped and hissed.

Scarlet got to her knees and the rest of them added blood to their elements. The youngest member cut her palm with a swift slice and held it over the fire. Blood gathered on the underside of her hand, and Clarabelle inhaled in preparation.

A bloody drop fell onto the fire, and the flames squealed and hissed in response.

Lily dropped her gaze to the book and began chanting in a foreign tongue. Hot, flickering flames grew higher as she spoke, and Clarabelle prayed to the Blessed Mother to watch over and protect them.

She sensed powerful darkness rising from the earth, creeping into her fingers, and throughout her hand before it traveled toward her heart. This ritual would change them all forever. She opened her heart to the darkness and let it flood her.

"So mote it be," Lily whispered, and the rest of them repeated the words in agreement.

"Seal it with blood," Lily instructed Scarlet.

She squeezed her hand together until another drop landed with a hiss and sizzled in the flames. A ripple of energy stole the breath from Clarabelle's lungs, and she struggled to get it back.

"Together now," Clarabelle said breathlessly, and the four of them clasped hands. "Blessed Mother, seal our wounds and bind us together. Let these spells stand until forever. We sisters together always will be. We ask of this, so mote it be."

The four witches got to their feet and kicked dirt over the fire to smother it. "Now, hurry home," Clarabelle said. "And speak of this to no one. When we can be sure the curse has worked, we will find a way to let it be known they have created a vile creature with their actions. Blessed be."

The others whispered the same and headed off in different directions.

Clarabelle raced through the darkening forest lest she be missed for being gone so long.

As she reached the town, she realized her fears had been for nothing. For a large commotion ensued in the street. When she drew closer, she realized the crying was for Mr. Braswell, a cruel man who had somehow impaled himself on a pitchfork.

CHAPTER ONE

Current Day

Hazel consulted the gadget on her wrist and then sent an annoyed look in Cora's direction. "I feel like a dog."

Cora turned a curiously disturbed look in her direction. "Huh?"

"I have to walk to get my treats. We've been out for nearly an hour, and I've only burned enough for one and a half cherry macaroons. Why is life so cruel?" Not to mention, the sun seemed extra hot today even though it was barely past ten a.m.

Cora snickered as she pumped her elbows to increase her workout. "Hasn't anyone told you, life isn't fair?"

"Well, it should be. If I get the chance, I'll be talking to the Blessed Mother about that one."

Cora grinned. "You do that. Just make sure it's not until you're really old."

"Then what's the point?" she said sarcastically. "If I'm ready to leave Earth, then it won't matter. I need someone to fix this now."

Her friend chuckled as they turned onto Camden Street. "Good luck with that one."

Hazel spied several people gathered on the church's lawn ahead and narrowed her gaze to see better. "What's going on at the old church?"

"Not sure," Cora said. "Let's find out."

As they neared, Hazel spotted the church's priest outside with Lobster Lucy standing next to a folding table and Mrs. Tillens seated on the only chair. She'd never had the unfortunate pleasure of meeting the priest, and instinct told her she didn't want to now.

Hazel slowed her stride. "Let's turn around."

Cora drew her brows together. "Why?"

"The priest is there, and I really don't want to be anywhere near him."

"Father Christopher?" She shrugged. "He's all right."

That didn't help her anxiety in the least. "He freaks me out. I'm afraid he's going to sense my magic, or the church will crumble if I go anywhere near it." It wasn't that she had an aversion to churches, just *this* church.

Cora's chuckle echoed through the stifling morning air.

Hazel came to a complete stop and turned her back to the church. "I'm serious. I get bad vibes from him."

"He's just a regular man, Hazel. He can't sense magic or read auras. If he did, they'd kick him out of the church."

"Maybe so, but don't forget Timothy Franklin has magic in his blood even though he doesn't claim it, and he secretly uses it against us. So, maybe the priest does, too, and we don't know it."

Cora slipped her arm through Hazel's and turned her around. "Don't let them scare you. We have just as much right to be in this town as they do. Plus, we have skills they don't."

Just because they had a right, didn't mean they should tempt fate.

"Come meet him, and you'll see."

Curiosity and peer pressure fought her common sense and won. She allowed Cora to pull her along until they neared the lush grass, and then she slipped her arm free.

Father Christopher, Mrs. Tillens, and Lobster Lucy all looked up as she and Cora approached. When the priest locked his eyes on Hazel, she gave him a hesitant smile. The older man with thinning gray hair and a skeletal figure returned the gesture, but something about him gave her chills.

Lobster Lucy waved. "Cora. We were just talking about you." The older, larger woman looked as salty and sturdy as some of the crews who came in off the fishing boats when they were docked near town.

"Me?" Cora joined the group, while Hazel remained closer to the fringe. "What about me?"

Mrs. Tillens, with her silver hair looking freshly washed and coiffed, gave Hazel a small wave, and she returned it.

Lucy thumbed toward the priest. "Father Christopher hoped we'd have a lot more people enter this year for the May Day Chowder Chowdown. I told him that I bet if I could convince you to join the fray, more people would enter. A few of the jealous women in town have bragged that they can cook better than you. If you sign up, I'll tell them they have the chance to prove it or shut up."

Cora put a hand over her mouth as if to hide her surprise. "Oh, I don't know about competing. I've never been one to enjoy that."

Hazel watched the priest while he studied Cora.

"It's for a good cause," he said. "And it will help with some of those black marks you've gotten for not attending church." His chuckle came off as hollow.

Cora blushed. "Sorry, Father. I have been a little lax about attending."

Hazel was surprised to learn that Cora would step foot in a church that didn't accept her beliefs. Hazel would refuse. She might not freely admit she was a witch, but she wouldn't pretend to be something she wasn't, either.

"Is that your acceptance then?" he pushed. "With all the rumors around town, it will do a body good to let others know where your loyalties lie."

Hazel quelled a gasp at his veiled threat. Be seen at church, or be labeled a witch, especially now. Anti-witch anxieties in modern times had hit an all-time high recently after the circulating rumors about Glenys and her behavior before her recent arrest for murder. But to use that as a scare tactic was deplorable.

"Of course, Father. I'd love to help out." Cora's reply might have seemed enthusiastic, but Hazel sensed the churning beneath. It was very reminiscent of her own thoughts. She'd bet Cora wished she'd listened to her when she'd said they should turn around.

Mrs. Tillens' sweet smile grew wide. "How about you, Hazel, dear? Wouldn't you love to help us out, too?"

The priest and Lobster Lucy turned their gazes on her, and her mind went blank. She'd be having words with Cora later. "Umm...I'm not one who enjoys clam chowder, so that's probably a bad idea. I doubt mine would be edible."

Lucy waved away her concerns with an over-sized hand. "We don't just make chowder, Hazel. You can enter the bread or dessert category."

"We could even start a new category for drinks," Mrs. Tillens added enthusiastically. "You could bring tea."

Father Christopher nodded. "As long as it's not peanut tea."

Hazel gave him a quizzical look. She'd never heard of a tea made from peanuts. She lifted her hands in a hold-it-right-there gesture. "I'm sorry, but it's really not my thing."

"What's not your thing," John Bartles asked as he joined the group. His sandy blond hair looked freshly cut, and his eyes emitted the usual friendliness. He was an everyday, average kind of guy. At least on the outside.

Hazel grew leery. "Entering competitions."

The priest extended his hand. "Good to see you, Officer Bartles."

John shook it with familiar friendliness that left her anxious.

John turned back to her. "You're going to deny the church when they need you?"

"Come on, Hazel," Mrs. Tillens encouraged. "We have a lot of fun, and you might find new customers."

Apparently, her options came down to two things. She could refuse and draw the attention of the town's witch hunters, or keep the enemy in sight, but be a hypocrite. She pasted on her best fake smile. "I do have some teas that are lovely over ice. I think they'd go perfectly with clam chowder."

The clapped his hands together. "Wonderful. I love it when a town comes together and supports the church. We all need God in our lives, and what better way to do it."

She worked to keep a smile in place. She wouldn't argue that having a higher power in one's life was a good thing, but this was no leader or man of God standing before her. His aura was too dirty for that.

"Wonderful." Mrs. Tillens' face beamed with pleasure. "I don't know why I haven't invited you to church before now, Hazel. People would love you, and you'd fit in so well."

"That's very kind of you to say." Hazel shot a glance at Cora and hoped her friend realized they needed to leave before they had her signed up for a baptism. "What's the date?"

"Next Sunday," Lucy supplied. "I'll be baking my incredibly delicious strawberry tarts. I'll have a special one just for you Father Christopher."

Mrs. Tillens scoffed. "Now, now, Lucy. That sounds a little like cheating."

Lucy frowned. "Does not."

The older lady offered a polite smile. "You're showing the judge special treatment."

Lucy slid the strap of her overalls higher on her shoulder. "Anyone else can do the same. I think Father Christopher can retain his impartiality. Don't you, Father?"

All gazes slid to the priest.

He reassured them with a nod. "I always do my best to be a fair and honest judge."

"See?" Lucy said to Mrs. Tillens with a sizeable amount of snark in her voice.

Mrs. Tillens pursed her lips and turned her gaze toward the papers in front of her. She wouldn't argue, but she obviously didn't agree. "Hazel and Cora, would you please write your names and what you're bringing?"

Hazel begrudgingly took the pen she offered and signed up for the contest. She turned and handed the pen to Cora with a sugary, you're-going-to-pay-for-this smile.

If Cora thought her sheepish expression would earn her any favors, she was dead wrong.

Cora wrote her name and then handed the pen to John Bartles. "Is your wife bringing her amazing chocolate cake again this year?"

He grinned. "Absolutely. That's why I'm here."

Hazel wanted to be snide and ask him what he himself was bringing, not his wife, since he'd contributed to her being railroaded, but it was best to stay on his good side until she had proof he wasn't part of the Sons of Stonebridge that would love to run her out of town. If they let her live that long.

"Susan's cake is my favorite." Cora nudged Hazel with her elbow. "Wait until you taste it."

"I'm looking forward to it." Though Hazel doubted very much that it could compete with Cora's cherry macaroons. She caught

Cora's attention. "We should probably get going. If I'm going to indulge in decadent chocolate cake, I'd better start burning more calories."

The group laughed.

Lucy stepped toward them. "I'll walk with you to the corner. See you later, John, Father Christopher." She didn't bother to say anything to Mrs. Tillens.

Hazel wanted to roll her eyes at their petty, small town drama but decided against it. She, apparently, was now one of the god-fearing citizens of Stonebridge. And everyone knew, good church-going people never acted that way.

She held back a snicker of laughter.

CHAPTER TWO

Lobster Lucy walked next to Cora on the sidewalk, while Hazel brought up the rear. She didn't mind. It gave her a chance to observe them both.

After Glenys' arrest for the murder of Belinda Atkins a couple of weeks ago, the whole town speculated about those Glenys had labeled the Damned. Which, in Stonebridge's terminology, meant "witch". Hazel wanted to know who was a legitimate witch as well, but for completely different reasons.

She'd kept her senses wide open for the first couple of days afterward, but picking up on everyone's emotions exhausted her. She'd have to discover them by other means.

Such as studying Lucy while she walked and talked to Cora.

Cora started pumping her elbows again as they picked up speed. "I'm surprised you're entering, Lucy. I thought you wanted nothing more to do with the church."

Hazel wanted to ask for more details regarding Lucy's decision, but she couldn't without being rude.

Lucy shrugged her large, sloped shoulders. "I got over it. Can't hold a grudge forever. Especially now that Ed's gone. I've put those horrible years behind me."

Cora dipped her head in acknowledgement. "Very wise words. You seem to be a lot happier these days, anyway. Why hold onto that baggage?"

"Dang straight," Lucy agreed. "I let that crap hit the road just like my ex-husband."

Hazel lifted her brows as the conversation turned juicier. In the few months since she'd arrived in Stonebridge, she had never heard that Lucy had been married before. The woman wasn't the least bit feminine, and she had a hard time picturing her with a man.

"Does that mean you're going to church again?" Cora asked.

Lucy snorted. "Isn't everybody? No one wants the damning finger pointed at them. I heard Glenys used your name." She glanced back at Hazel. "Yours, too."

"Isn't that the dumbest thing?" Cora chuckled. "Poor gal. She obviously was out of her mind. I mean, a sane person wouldn't commit murder."

Lucy gave her a firm nod. "Not without a good reason. She didn't like Belinda, but that wasn't a reason to kill her. Also, you and Hazel are some of the nicest people in town. You couldn't possibly be witches. I hope Glenys gets the help she needs."

They stopped at the corner where Lucy would part ways with them. The hefty woman regarded them with a cheeky grin. "You both should come with me next Sunday. We can sit together."

"I can't," Hazel said without hesitation, and the other women turned to her with questions in their eyes. "My mother is coming to visit." Which was about the biggest lie she could tell if Hazel had her way, but her mom was the only excuse she could think of quickly.

"Then come to church the week after. By then, everyone will be excited and talking about the results of the cook off. Seeing as I'll be one of the winners, I should probably go." She gave them a conspiratorial wink.

"Sure," Cora said. "I'll get someone to cover the morning shift. Hazel?"

If she kept refusing, people would take a serious, second look at her. "Sure. Sounds lovely."

With a satisfied nod, Lucy left them and strode across the street. When she was out of distance, Hazel gave a low growl. "I may hex you for this."

Cora tightened her features into a guilty look. "Sorry. I didn't know what else to do. But it's just church. Half the people only go because it's expected anyway."

"I've never sat through a service in my life," Hazel countered. "And now I have to."

"I have to go, too," Cora said with a fair amount of misery.

"Yes, but it sounds like you've submitted willingly to this before. If you hadn't, you wouldn't know Father Christopher, and he would have never been able to coerce you into going because you wouldn't have talked to him. But now, because of your crazy actions, I have to go, too."

Cora held her gaze for a long moment, trying to look contrite and failing, before a small smile cracked her face. "It's only church. It won't kill you."

Hazel rolled her eyes. "When thunder strikes the building and it's falling on our heads, I'm going to tell you I told you so."

Cora laughed then. "Deal. Until then, be glad they consider you one of them. The alternative would be much worse."

She supposed it would, but it was hard to think that right now.

Maybe the building would collapse before that Sunday arrived. It was ancient, after all.

CHAPTER THREE

Hazel enjoyed the show of muscle as Police Chief Peter Parrish hefted glass dispensers full of her summertime blends of teas and placed them in the small wagon. Afterward, she'd let him help her haul them to her assigned table on the church grounds.

The strawberry, apple and lemon grass green tea was her favorite that she'd created so far, but she really enjoyed the peach herbal tea, too. She was sure the people of Stonebridge would love them.

Hazel led the way across the lawn decorated with banners and balloons, pulling a chest full of ice. An excited energy filled the air as children danced around the May Day pole. People milled about and set up other tasting stations, and she had to admit she liked the positive atmosphere.

Not to mention, the gorgeous old church and meticulous grounds appealed to her artistic senses. She'd have to give Father Christopher credit for keeping the lawn and gardens beautiful.

Though, if it were up to her, she'd plant a few more flowers.

She pointed toward a small table as she and Peter neared it. "That one's mine."

Peter waited while she unfolded and spread the bright yellow tablecloth adorned with pink and white hibiscus. The cheerful flowers always brought a smile when she used it.

When she was finished, he lifted one of the dispensers and set it on the table. "Is that where you want it?"

The look on his face begged her to say yes, and she knew why. The full containers were beyond heavy. There had been no way she could have carried them on her own.

"That's perfect. Thank you."

She couldn't say she minded having the town's hot police chief as her boyfriend.

She also couldn't say their relationship was back to normal because they hadn't talked about what had taken place in his office that fateful day when she'd had to cast a spell on Glenys to keep her under control.

His gaze collided with hers. "Anything to help out the church."

She kept her expression passive until the corner of his mouth quirked upward, causing her to smile. "Yes, whatever Father Christopher needs."

He'd managed to keep the priest off his tail for not attending by using work as an excuse. The father protected the town's souls, while Peter protected their lives. A complementary duo, Peter had explained to her.

She had a feeling that deep down, he wasn't interested in attending any more than she was. "If you wouldn't mind getting the other two dispensers, I'll get the rest of my booth set up."

He gave her a nod of agreement. "Are you charging for tea? Some put donation jars on their tables."

She glanced about the growing number of townsfolk arriving at the church. "I'd kind of hoped to use this to make friends with people I haven't met, yet. What better way to make them happy than give them something free. Then, if they like it, they can come to the teashop and purchase more."

"They'll like you, too. Not just your tea. Hard to point fingers at someone they really like."

She grinned, not surprised he'd seen right through her tactics. "You're too smart for your own good."

"So are you." His smile stoked the fire burning inside her. "I'll be right back."

She watched the heart-stealing man stroll back across the lawn, waving in greeting at those he passed. Never in a million years would she have believed she could tell him she was a witch and think he could still care about her.

But he did.

That made her like him even more.

Cora called it love, said the threads of their tapestry grew stronger every day. She didn't know about that, but she did love the way he made her feel when he was around.

Tons of people visited her table during the next hour. Luckily, Peter stayed by her side to help. When Mrs. Tillens and Mrs. Lemon popped by for cups of peach herbal iced tea, Hazel grilled Mrs. Tillens, asking why there were no other booths with drinks available.

Mrs. Tillens guiltily admitted she'd forgotten to advertise the category but promised Hazel would have won anyway.

That wasn't the point.

When Hazel's last dispenser was half-empty, she eyed the priest sitting at the table of honor. He had yet to visit her and try the tea. "I think Father Christopher is avoiding me."

Peter glanced toward the priest. "Why do you say that?"

"He hasn't come over once. You'd think he would after all the pressuring he gave me." Well, Cora really. But, she'd felt it all the same.

He chuckled. "He waits until everyone has sampled and then contestants are supposed to present their entries to him. He's just sitting down now, and that's probably the signal that he's ready."

She lowered her lids into a sardonic stare. "You're kidding, right? We're supposed to present him with gifts like he's a king?"

Enjoyment twinkled in his eyes. "You want him to like you, don't you?"

"Not especially," she grumbled and begrudgingly filled a plastic cup with ice and tea. "I'm not waiting until everyone else lines up to please the magistrate. He can have it now or die waiting. I don't know why I agreed to this in the first place."

He shrugged and gave her a sarcastic look. "I think we both know the answer to that."

She huffed her annoyance, pasted on a smile, and left Peter in charge of things while she made the pilgrimage to the table of honor.

Father Christopher greeted her with a pleasant smile. He was clearly in his element, enjoying all the attention. She had to wonder if this was for his ego instead of to raise money for the church.

"Hello, Father Christopher," she said brightly. "I bring you my offering." She placed it before him on the table and dipped in curtsy.

He laughed. "Thank you, my child. I'm sure I will love it."

"Here's mine, too," Lucy said, coming up behind her. "If Hazel's not waiting until the official time, then neither am I."

She widened her eyes innocently. "Oh, sorry. I didn't realize there was an official time."

The priest waved away her worries. "Not a problem. After we all spoke the other day, I've been eagerly waiting to taste your tea and Lobster Lucy's strawberry tart. If they are as good as you claim, I won't need to sample anything else."

Hazel wanted to point out that as a judge, he was required to taste all the entries and he'd promised impartiality, but she kept her snarky comments to herself.

She should have been honored that he chose to sample her iced tea first, but really, she couldn't care less what he thought. This was all for show.

He lifted the cup to his lips and savored the sip as though he was tasting a fine wine. "Excellent," he said and smiled, and then took another drink.

He winked at Hazel, making her skin crawl. "Now, let's try this tasty tart, shall we?"

Before he sunk his fork through the flaky crust, a wave of nausea rolled through her. Not the regular nausea she encountered when she was in the presence of a smarmy guy, but something more sinister circling around them.

An overwhelming urge to tell him not to eat or drink anything else surged inside her. But if she said something, he'd question her reason, and then she might as well sign her death warrant.

She held her breath as he took a bite, chewed, and then gave Lobster Lucy the same smile. "Perfection. I shouldn't have expected otherwise."

Lucy preened over the praise, while Hazel exhaled in relief. She'd worried for nothing. She'd also had quite enough of his preening.

"Thank you very much, Father. I'm pleased you enjoyed it." She glanced over her shoulder toward Peter who watched with an annoying smile on his face. "I should probably get back to my table. I left Chief Parrish in charge, and who knows what he might do."

Father Christopher laughed and dismissed her with a nod as a king might do to a peasant.

When she was close enough that no one would see but Peter, she rolled her eyes. "Unbelievable," she whispered and joined him behind the table.

"He's definitely in his element."

"I'd say."

A piercing scream cut through their chitchat and drove a stake of terror into her heart. She looked toward the sound and discovered Father Christopher clutching at his throat and reaching out toward the crowd with his other.

"He's choking," someone yelled.

"He needs his Epi Pen," another called out.

Mrs. Tillens jumped up from a nearby table. "I'll get it." She hurried off toward the church as fast as her elderly legs would carry her.

Many rushed forward, blocking Hazel's view.

Peter placed a hand in front of her chest, preventing her from moving. "Stay here." Then he rushed toward the crowd.

She paused for half a second. "As if," she muttered and then followed him.

CHAPTER FOUR

The crowd swallowed Peter before Hazel could catch up to him. She nudged between the townsfolk, slowly making her way to the ailing priest amidst cries of "Help him!" and "Do the Heimlich maneuver".

She finally squeezed into a position where she could see the priest slumped over the table, his face squashing the delightful strawberry tart Lucy had just presented to him. If the bluish tinge to his face was any indication, she knew he didn't have much time. If any.

"I need everyone to take a giant step back," Peter commanded.

They all did, including Hazel.

With the help of another man, Peter laid Father Christopher out on the grass and tilted his head back to open his airway. Some folks chose to leave, while the more curious ones like her stayed to gawk.

Someone gripped her elbow, and Hazel turned to find Cora clutching her and watching the disturbing scene before them. "What happened?" she whispered.

Hazel shook her head. "I'm not sure. He was completely fine a few moments ago when Lucy and I presented him with our offerings. I'd barely made it back to my table when this all happened. Sounds like some people think he had an allergic reaction, or he choked on something."

Mrs. Lemon joined them. She clucked her tongue, and Hazel thought it was fitting since she sported a ridiculous cotton-stuffed chicken on top. "It's the May Day Curse."

Hazel drew her brows together. "May Day Curse? What does that mean?"

Cora nodded solemnly. "Every forty years, someone dies on May first. I've heard that it's happened consistently since olden times, but I didn't really believe it. Until now."

Hazel scoffed. "Every forty years? Isn't it likely that it's a naturally occurring phenomenon?" The town was notorious for looking for reasons to blame witches for bad things.

Mrs. Lemon adjusted her hat, tilting it so the stuffed didn't lean so far to the right. "People drop like clockwork. I don't remember who died when I was ten years old. But when I was fifty, I certainly remember that crazy old coot, Jefferson, when, out of the blue, he tripped on the sidewalk and split his head wide open."

The chicken's feet hanging off the edge of her hat momentarily distracted Hazel. She blinked and refocused. "Someone dies the first of May every forty years?"

Cora and Mrs. Lemon both nodded.

The older woman took her hand and squeezed. "Don't worry dear. You'll be in your sixties before it happens again, and it likely won't be you. I'll be dead and buried, so I won't have to worry about it killing me."

Hazel lifted a confused brow. Had the sweet, little lady just told her that being dead would save her from dying?

Cora caught her eye and shook her head as though to encourage her to let the comment lie.

Mrs. Tillens called out and hurried their way. *"I've got the Epi Pen!"*

From what Hazel could tell, there wasn't much hope for the Father, and her heart broke for the dear old lady and what she was about to discover.

Sirens screamed through the once-quiet, sunny day, and the crowd further dispersed. Paramedics rushed forward and took over for Peter.

By then, Peter's men had also assembled. "Give Father Christopher his privacy," Officer John Bartles said and forced them to move away.

"Oh, goodness." Mrs. Lemon pointed toward Mrs. Tillens who now sat at a table not far from poor Father Christopher, her face ashen and one hand over her heart. A medic knelt in front of her, checking her pulse. "I'd better get to Iris. She's not faring so well."

"Of course," Hazel said. She considered offering her assistance but knew she'd be in the way. "What a horrible day."

Hazel walked with Cora toward their tables. As they did, she leaned close enough to whisper. "Seriously, how many bad things are they going to blame on innocent witches?"

"Oh, plenty," Cora responded. "There's the time when lightning cancelled the town's baseball playoffs. The year we ended up with a pothole in the road the size of Texas. Okay, it really wasn't that big, but it was bad."

Cora paused to glance over her shoulder before continuing. "Most accusations aren't true, but there is one that I believe is. Stonebridge will never be able to remove all magic from town. The curse proclaimed that at least one descendant from each of the original witches will always reside here."

Hazel also glanced toward the commotion still ensuing over Father Christopher's body to ensure no one paid attention to them or their conversation. "A descendant from all of the witches?" She boxed one of her glass tea containers.

Cora began to disassemble another of them. "That's right. Glenys descends from Eliza. Belinda was from Scarlet. Timothy from Lily."

The conversation swerved in a direction Hazel hadn't anticipated, and she swallowed the rising lump in her throat, thinking about her own witch grandmother, Clarabelle. Cora hadn't mentioned her relative. If Hazel didn't ask, that would be obvious and awkward. And if she did...the same.

Guilt poured over her like freezing rain for not being a better friend. "Clarabelle's offspring?"

Cora gave her a pointed look, and Hazel realized that she already knew.

"Is me," Hazel finished and put the final tea container in its box.

She nodded.

If she wanted her new friends to trust her, she needed to start trusting them, too. Cora had been nothing but loyal and kind to her. "How long have you known?"

Cora snorted and slid the bright yellow and pink cloth from the table to fold. "Since her cat took up residence at your house. Remember? We talked about it, though we didn't say it in so many words. I thought you knew that I knew."

She hadn't. "But having that darned cat stalk me didn't necessarily make me a direct descendant." Did it? There was so much about this town and her history that she didn't know.

"Trust me. Many a witch have tried to get him to become their familiar. He's a particularly discerning cat, and there's no other reason he'd choose you."

"He's a royal pain in the butt, is what he is." Although, he had come through for her recently. Still, she hated to give him too much credit and puff up his already huge ego and snarky attitude. "Why didn't you say something sooner?"

Cora tucked the tablecloth into Hazel's bag, and Hazel added the leftover plastic cups. "I didn't want to rush you. From what I gathered, you knew none of this before coming to Stonebridge. I figured we had time to work our way through things."

Hazel paused cleaning up and met Cora's gaze. "I wish I felt like I had time. It seems like everything is coming at me full speed."

"Once again, I'll say that your mother and grandmother did you a huge disservice by not telling you these things."

Hazel drew a strand of hair across her lips as she thought back through her childhood and early adult years, searching for clues she might have missed. "I'm not sure they knew anything, either. There's nothing I can pinpoint that says, ha, you should have seen this coming."

"Maybe that explains why we've waited so long to have someone from Clarabelle's line to complete the circle."

Each of them picked up a box and headed toward Peter's truck, thoughts still percolating in Hazel's mind. She knew he'd be at the scene for a while, so he'd have to drop off her stuff later. She could walk home or catch a ride with Cora, but not with all her boxes, too.

She lifted a container into Peter's truck and frowned. "But I thought the curse said someone from each line would always live in Stonebridge. Who was the one before me then? Was the curse wrong?"

"I'm not sure. Maybe if you didn't know about your heritage, then other witches didn't either. Maybe someone was here all along and recently left."

Maybe none of them would ever know.

The chaos surrounding Father Christopher increased as they lifted him onto a gurney. She'd like to feel bad that the priest was no longer a physical being, but the vibes from him that she'd encountered weren't good. Instinct told her the citizens would be better off without him, and that was a sad thing.

"Does Father Christopher have any family that we know of?" Hazel could feel empathy for those folks.

"I believe he has a brother in New York, but they were never close. He's the only person I ever heard Father Christopher talk about."

Hazel couldn't say she was surprised.

She stepped closer to Cora. "Can I tell you something?"

Her friend nodded.

"I'm almost certain I felt something weird happening when I was at Father Christopher's table. Like a warning or something."

Instead of responding, Cora shifted her gaze away from Hazel and stiffened.

Hazel turned to see what had stolen her attention. Officer Bartles strode toward them, and Hazel's anxiety rocketed straight to fight or flight mode. The usual smile he wore was missing and had been replaced by something darker.

Hazel made sure to mask her features as well. "Hello, John."

"Cora. Hazel." He nodded to each of them. "Hazel, I need to ask you to come to the station with me for questioning."

Unwanted surprise burst inside her. "Me? What for?"

Officer Bartles studied her with an intensity that left her leery. "It appears that Father Christopher may have met with foul play, and you were one of the last to speak to him."

"Foul play?" She took a step back. "I only delivered a glass of tea to him. I barely know the man."

He gave her a curt nod. "I understand. Please, if you'll accompany me?"

Hazel glanced at Cora before searching for Peter amongst the crowd. Someone needed to talk sense into Officer Bartles. "I'm sorry, John. I feel like maybe you received bad information or misunderstood. I had nothing to do with Father Christopher's death."

His lips curved into a kind smile. "Hazel. I don't doubt that you're innocent, but certain circumstances, which we won't be discussing here, require that I question you. I'm only doing my job." He held out a hand to indicate she should step forward.

She wasn't sure why her heart pounded in uneven thumps. She had nothing to hide. But even a hint of wrongdoing on her part left her sick. "Does Peter know about this?"

He gave her another condescending smile that rubbed like a pebble in her shoe. "Yes, ma'am. This is standard procedure. The sooner we go, the sooner you can get back to your life. Assuming, you know, that you're innocent." He winked, which she didn't find funny at all.

She glanced once more at Cora and then tossed up her hands in defeat. "Let's go then."

She walked with John in stony silence toward the street where several Stonebridge Police Department SUVs and cruisers had parked. He opened the passenger door of the SUV on the corner, and she climbed in, fuming. What a waste of taxpayer dollars.

From the corner of her eye, she caught sight of Peter striding across the church lawn toward John with an unhappy look on his face. John headed toward him.

If body language was any indication, Peter had not been fully aware of John's activities. Peter gestured toward where Hazel waited and then pointed a stern finger at John's chest.

Satisfaction spread through her like warm honey. She wasn't sure exactly what Peter was saying, but she knew he was defending her, and she liked it.

The sound of a loud engine and screeching tires drew her gaze to the front windshield. She turned in time to see the black blur of a small, two-door hatchback careen wildly around the corner, overcorrect, and head straight in her direction.

Instinctively, she closed her eyes.

The car hit with enough force to slam her against the passenger door. Tiny squares of glass rained from the driver's side window as metal crunched in response.

She fought to catch her breath. The sound of her thundering heart filled the space around her.

Then people yelling pierced her reality as though her ears had begun working again. The passenger door jerked open, and Peter reached in with strong arms and surrounded her.

"Are you okay?" he said with emotion clinging to his words.

She hesitated and then nodded. Besides the fright, she didn't think she'd sustained any damage. Except maybe she'd bumped the side of her head.

None of it made sense right now.

Peter pulled her from the vehicle into a world of chaos. Officers left Father Christopher with one of the paramedics, and the rest of the first responders raced past her and into the road.

The front end of the black vehicle had been firmly planted into the side of the police SUV. The windshield on the driver's side was cracked like a spider web radiating out from a center point that appeared to be bloody.

She wanted to do something, say something, but her body resisted.

A crew of officers opened the driver's door, and from the looks on their faces, she knew the outcome was bad.

"Hazel!" Cora raced toward her. "Oh, my stars." She looked her over frantically. "You're okay. You're okay."

"Stay with her," Peter commanded and then peered into Hazel's eyes. "I need to assess the situation. Let Cora take you to the medical center."

"I'm..." She was surprised to find her words shaky. "I'm okay."

He glanced over her head to Cora. "Make sure someone looks at her. Take her to the medic over there if nothing else. Then take her home, please."

Hazel fought to keep her head clear. "What about the questioning?"

Peter gave her a pointed look. "It can wait."

Cora nodded and then wrapped an arm about Hazel's waist and led her away. "There's nothing we can do here but pray to the Blessed Mother. It seems the curse has taken two from us this year. We're lucky it wasn't three."

CHAPTER FIVE

An hour after Hazel crashed on her couch with an ice pack across her forehead, someone rang her doorbell. She didn't move or open her eyes. After the day she'd had, she wanted nothing more to do with the outside world.

Unfortunately, she could hear Cora cross the carpet and step onto her tiled entryway. The door squeaked as she opened it, and Hazel made a mental note to oil the hinges as soon as she could care about anything again.

Which might not be for a long time.

"Hazel here?" Officer Bartles' voice carried across the room.

She would have cringed if it wouldn't have made her head hurt.

Nevertheless, she actually liked John. Had since she'd first met him when she'd shared a hamburger meal with him and Peter at the police station.

She couldn't hate him, even though she couldn't reconcile finding his signature on the Sons of Stonebridge document proclaiming his vow to destroy witches with same the man who often smiled at her.

She would be careful around him, though.

"She's resting," Cora said with a fair amount of annoyance in her voice.

"Awful thing, that accident this afternoon. I'm glad she's okay. If Peter hadn't stopped me, I might have been victim number three for the day."

"Or Hazel could have been, too." Cora's implication that it was John's fault that Hazel had been in the vehicle and therefore part of the accident came through loud and clear.

"Exactly." He sighed, obviously missing her point. "We can thank God we're okay."

"Amen," Cora agreed, bringing a small smile to Hazel's face, knowing that wasn't a word she typically used.

A long pause ensued and then John released a heavy sigh. "Come on, Cora. I'm just doing my job. She was with Father Christopher moments before he died, and he didn't pass from natural causes."

More silence, and Hazel wondered if Cora was giving him the raised eyebrow, I-don't-care look, or if she'd chosen the more severe, narrow-eyed, I'm-likely-to-hurt-you look that she sometimes used on unruly customers. She'd like to think it was the latter.

"Don't make me be a jerk, Cora. Just because I'm questioning her doesn't mean I think she's guilty. Heck, I like Hazel. A lot. But maybe she saw something, you know? She was right there."

Hazel groaned as she sat up and placed the ice pack on a nearby table. "I'm coming, John."

Everything ached. If she hadn't tensed during the impact, she would have been just fine. But...hindsight. And really, she doubted there were many who could have gone with the flow and stayed relaxed in that same situation.

He gave her a sheepish grin as she approached. "Sorry, Hazel. You know I don't like to do this." Friendliness remained his main emotion, but she sensed something darker lurking beneath.

She gave him a brief nod. "I'll go willingly if you can promise me ibuprofen and a caffeine-infused drink once we get there."

She should have thought earlier to pull out the muscle salve she'd created. She'd definitely use it as soon as she was back home.

He smiled and held out his arm. "Deal."

She turned to Cora. "I'll call you when I'm finished, okay?"

Cora cast a nasty glance at John and then turned to Hazel. "You'd better. I can come right back over, too, if you need me."

"I'll be fine. But thank you."

John held the door for them before he stepped out and closed it behind him.

Hazel hadn't seen hide nor hair of Mr. Kitty since she'd come home, and she was glad he hadn't chosen that moment to make an appearance. She supposed she needed to give him credit for being smarter than she'd first thought.

Hazel clicked her seatbelt into place as John climbed into the driver's seat of what appeared to be Peter's car. "Chief let you take his vehicle?"

He buckled up and started the engine. "Yeah. Mine's not drivable."

No kidding. Part of her wished she could get another look at both cars now that fear and adrenaline no longer clouded her brain. "I'm guessing you've identified the driver of the other vehicle. Can you tell me who it was?"

Sadness dimmed his aura, and he put the car in drive. "Karen Bernard. Something of a loner. Worked in Salem and kept to herself for the most part. Never saw her at church."

Hazel shifted a sideways glance toward him. "You never see me there, either."

He grinned. "I've noticed. Doesn't mean you won't at some point, though."

She wanted to argue that, yeah, it probably did, but now wasn't the time. "I heard a couple of people blame today's tragedies on a curse."

"The May Day Curse."

She waited for a snicker or hint of doubt, but none came. "Do you believe it's true?"

He tapped his fingers against the steering wheel. "It seems crazy to think such a thing could be true, but we have at least one unexplained death on the exact date as the curse, which has apparently happened in the past, and yes, I do believe the evil witches in Stonebridge's past have cursed our town in other ways, so why not this one, too? That's why I believe it's important to not let them nest here again."

Nest? She crinkled her forehead. "You make it sound like an infestation." Which horrified her more than a little.

"If we let them take over, that's what it will be." He pulled in front of the police station and killed the engine. "Don't worry, Hazel. I know that what happened this afternoon was scary...for both of us, but we'll keep you safe."

She fought not to roll her eyes in disgust.

"Even as we speak, Timothy is searching the library records. He seems to think there might be something in one of them that can prove who's a witch and who isn't. He thought holy water and maybe something else. I'm sure he'll let us know as soon as he finds it."

Timothy Franklin had become more of a thorn in her side than she'd thought possible. "If he's so smart, why doesn't he already know?" After all, he was an expert on witches.

John snorted. "Good point." He opened his door, and she didn't wait for him to get hers. Together, they walked up the steps into the police station.

Margaret in reception was almost unrecognizable wearing her hair pinned up with a chopstick, pale makeup and bright red lips. Her red silk kimono with intricate black and gold designs looked incredible, if a little out of place. On a different day, Hazel would have been beyond jealous of its luxuriant beauty.

Margaret caught her gaze as they approached and shifted an unhappy expression toward John. "Officer Bartles."

His shoulders slumped. "Geez, Margaret. Would you all lighten up? We have to interrogate her."

"Interrogate?" Margaret challenged. "You mean question, right?"

He waved an impatient hand. "Yes, Margaret. That's what I meant. Which room is open?"

"The first one. When you're done *interrogating* poor Hazel, equally poor Lucy is waiting in the next one."

John snatched a yellow notepad from the corner of Margaret's desk and then led the way to the interview room. Hazel glanced toward Peter's empty office as they walked.

Once in the room, John closed the door behind them. "Have a seat."

Hazel warily claimed a blue, formed-plastic chair on one side of the plain, utilitarian table. When John placed the pad on the table between them and sat opposite her, all moisture in her mouth evaporated.

She glanced toward the one-way glass and searched the atmosphere for Peter's essence, but she couldn't sense him.

John cleared his throat and drew her attention. "I only have a few questions for you, Hazel."

She nodded.

"How well did you know Father Christopher?"

She shrugged. "Not at all really. I met him a few days ago when he coerced Cora into joining the Chowder Chowdown. You showed up just after that to sign up for your wife to bring her cake."

His brows shot up. "Coerced? Did Cora have problems with him?"

"No. Of course not. I just meant that he'd pressured her. You know, using the town's fear of witches and saying if she supported the church she wouldn't have to worry."

"Does she support the church?"

Her answers seemed to be a futile grasp on a very slippery slope. She realized she could answer honestly and cost her friend and herself a ton of trouble, or she could lie. "Of course, she does, John. She mentioned to me not long ago that her business had been struggling, so I'm sure she's working more Sundays, and that's probably why she hasn't been in attendance."

He narrowed his gaze. "What about you? Did you have issues with Father Christopher? Do you believe in God?"

They were hardly the same thing.

She forced an embarrassed smile. "You know, new girl to town, bad experience with my previous church. Lucy invited us, though, to go with her."

His intensity released, and he smiled. "That's great. We'd love to have you join us at church. My wife keeps saying she'd like to know Peter's girl better."

She did manage a genuine smile then. "I'd like that, too. Cora can't say enough good things about her."

"She's a real gem, my Susan. Lucky was the day she agreed to marry me."

Hazel smiled, hoping that would be the end of their session.

"What about Lucy?" he continued. "She hasn't been to church much for a long time, and she said some unkind things about Father Christopher while he was counseling her and her husband a while back. Apparently, she believed he'd sided with her husband unfairly."

Hazel widened her eyes. "I really don't know anything about that. It all happened before I moved to Stonebridge."

He nodded. "You said you saw Lucy the day you signed up. Did she seem all right then?"

"Yeah. She was great. In fact, she was excited to share her strawberry tart with Father Christopher. Mrs. Tillens commented that it might be cheating to bribe the judge by serving him an extra big piece, but it all seemed in good fun."

John nodded as he wrote. Then he pierced her with another sharp look, leaned back in his chair, and sighed. "I'll be honest with you, Hazel. You and Lucy are our main suspects at this point."

She placed her fists and elbows on the table. "That is utterly ridiculous. Based on what evidence?"

He lifted a shoulder and let it drop. "Father Christopher died from anaphylactic shock. Everyone knows he has a severe peanut allergy."

"I didn't know that," she shot back. But she did recall him mentioning something about peanut tea.

"Lucy's strawberry tart and your tea were the only things he'd eaten recently."

She shook her head repeatedly. "That's...that's...that's ludicrous. I didn't do it, and I can't believe she did. Neither of us had motive."

"That we know of."

She sat staring at him, speechless. Her? A prime suspect in a murder case? "What if someone is trying to frame one of us?"

He lifted his brows, seeming interested in her theory. "Do you have reason to believe someone might?"

She bit her bottom lip as she tried frantically to think up a reason. The only thing she could come up with was her heritage, but Peter and Cora were the only ones in town who knew.

She hoped.

"I don't know, John. I just know it wasn't me."

The door to the interview room opened, and Peter stepped in. "I think she's answered all your questions, John. You might want to let her know that we're having Father Christopher's food and drink tested to check for traces of peanut or other toxins. If she's innocent, she has nothing to worry about."

Officer Bartles looked as though he wanted to argue but nodded instead. "Yes. I guess we're good. For now. Don't leave town, Hazel."

"John," Peter warned.

Hazel shot him a disturbed look. "I have no reason to leave. I'm innocent."

John nodded, and Peter gestured with a jerk of his head for her to follow him.

She didn't look at John as she left, afraid whatever look she gave him would only make things worse for her.

CHAPTER SIX

Peter firmly took Hazel's hand and guided her toward the doors leading out of the police station. The feel of his strong fingers wrapped possessively around hers did wonders for her weary spirit.

"I'm headed home for the day," he said to Margaret.

She flashed Hazel a big grin. "Yes, sir. Have a good evening."

"It's got to be better than today," he mumbled.

After that, he remained silent until they were both settled in his truck with her cook-off supplies still hanging out in the truck bed. "I can't believe that guy." Anger broke with each of his syllables. *"Who does he think he is?"*

The ferocity of his tone made her shiver. It also warmed her insides. She liked to think she was a strong, independent woman, but she did like knowing her man would fight for her. "He was probably just trying to do his job." Though she didn't really believe that, either.

"He's going to be lucky if he has a job when this is all said and done. The second the lab clears your name, he's going to be scrubbing toilets."

She tugged one of his rigid hands from the steering wheel and twined her fingers between his. "Thank you."

He cast a quick glance in her direction and then heaved a sigh. "What a nightmare. It's bad enough we're investigating two deaths. Bartles doesn't need to be dragging you into the middle of it."

"How long does it take the lab to test?"

He slowed and then parked in front of her house. "Not long for initial testing. I had two of my men take the items to the state lab to avoid all possible suggestions of tampering. I want this over and without any chance of nasty, untrue rumors pointed in your direction."

She and Peter might have their share of problems, but she couldn't have picked a more decent guy. Err...allowed him to pick her, that was. "Thank you for watching out for me. I can't imagine how big this nightmare might be without you on my side."

He shut off the engine and shifted in his seat to fully look at her. "I'm doing this for you, but not only you. I want this investigation handled properly, without the silliness of the May Day Curse or inept officers messing it up."

She tilted her head, surprised by his vehemence. "Does that mean you don't believe in the curse?"

His eyes looked harder than green aventurines. "I believe there's a logical reason behind both of the deaths today. I can't say Karen Bernard's wasn't an accident, but some crazy curse didn't force her to crash into Bartle's vehicle."

As much as she wondered if her long-ago grandmother might have had something to do with the incidents today, she liked Peter's version of events much better. "I hope you find the answers soon."

"Me, too. Let's get you inside. I'll drop off the stuff in the back of my truck at your shop tomorrow morning."

She relaxed against the seat and watched him walk around the front of the truck to open her door. He held out a hand to help her out. She smiled when he kept his fingers wrapped tight around hers as they walked to the front door.

Once inside, she dropped the house keys on the table near the door and kicked off her shoes. Every part of her was exhausted. "John promised me ibuprofen and caffeine if I went to the station with him, and he never followed through." She said it in a teasing tone though she wished she'd had the forethought to remind him. She might be feeling a lot better now.

Peter grunted his disappointment. "Another black mark against him. This might very well be the worst day in his career."

She placed a hand on his cheek. "Don't be too hard on him. He's been a good officer, otherwise, right? Maybe he just needs more training."

He pulled her tight against him, and she reveled in the feel of his body heat soaking into hers. "I'd tell you what he needs, but my thoughts aren't meant for a lady's ears."

She grinned at him and tugged his head toward hers. "Come here."

He captured her lips and suddenly all was right with the world again. She let him kiss away her worries, never intending to stop him.

When he pulled away, she sighed at her loss.

"I don't think you should have caffeine this late at night. It will keep you up, and you obviously need your sleep. You'll likely feel worse in the morning." He glanced toward the kitchen. "Do you have any muscle relaxers?"

She shook her head.

He gave her a stern look. "You should have gone to the doctor like I suggested."

She frowned. "I wasn't hurting this bad earlier. I'll rub on some of my salve like I used on you, and that will help."

His lips curved into a grin. "That stuff is amazing. Made with magic?"

She rolled her eyes. "No. It's all herbal."

He pondered for a moment and then nodded. "Tell me where it is. I'll get it and pay back the favor."

She caught his gaze with a quizzical one of her own. He had to realize what the feel of his strong hands on her bare skin would do to her, didn't he? Then again, he'd probably enjoy that very much.

Still, she wasn't dumb enough to resist something that would help her feel tons better. "Top shelf of my medicine cabinet. White jar with the blue lid."

She followed him down the hall and opened the door to her bedroom as he stepped into the bathroom. "Give me a moment, and I'll meet you in the living room."

She moved to her dresser where she pulled out a tank top and flannel bottoms that she wore to lounge around the house. He couldn't very well rub her shoulders in the blouse she currently wore, and she wasn't about to take off her shirt like he had.

Back in the living room, she found him waiting next to the couch. "Sit here and face the kitchen."

She did as he asked, sitting with her back against the armrest, giving him full access. A shiver raced over her before he ever touched her skin. She realized it was only a massage, but other than kissing and hugging, it was the most intimate they'd been.

She involuntarily gasped as his fingers connected with her shoulders and slid her straps down. She swore her skin sizzled where he touched.

"You okay?"

She nodded as he pressed and rubbed her neck. "Yeah. Just..." She didn't bother to finish her sentence but dropped her chin to her chest instead, hoping she didn't start purring like Mr. Kitty. Well, maybe he wasn't the best reference for purring, but he had that one time.

"Let me know if I push too hard," he murmured.

She relaxed as his hands warmed and stretched her stiff muscles. The feel of his skin on hers lulled her into a sleepy state, and she closed her eyes to focus solely on his touch.

"Hazel?" Peter's voice was awfully close to her ear, and she opened her eyes with a start.

"Yes?" She blinked a few times to pull her back into the present.

He chuckled softly. "I think you fell asleep." He walked to the front of the couch and peered down at her.

Embarrassment heated her cheeks. "No, I didn't. I was just really relaxed."

His smile grew bigger. "Uh-huh. I think maybe my job is done, and you should head to bed."

She gave him a sleepy smile. "Your fingers are amazing."

He snorted. "So, I've been told."

She lifted teasing brows, and he held up a hand. "Forget I said that. Do you want me to help you to your room?"

She placed a hand on her cheek and rested her chin in her palm. "I think that's a really good idea and a really bad one."

He gave her a knowing nod. "Right. I'll just see myself out then and see you in the morning at your shop." He held out a hand and helped her from the couch.

She leaned into him and soaked up the pleasure from a long kiss. "Goodnight, Peter. Thank you for taking care of me."

He held her gaze for a long, delicious moment. "My pleasure."

It took all her will not to ask him to stay. "I'll see you tomorrow?"

"Sure. First thing. You can make me some tea."

She smiled, loving his dark, wavy hair and devastating green eyes. "I'd love to."

He headed to the door and then paused to look back at her. After a second, he shifted his gaze to the carpet near her feet. "You take care of her, okay?"

Hazel found Mr. Kitty sitting beneath the coffee table watching them, and she widened her eyes and smiled. He released a long meow that made Peter chuckle.

"I don't think he likes me much."

Hazel snorted. "Don't worry. That's what he always says to me, too."

He dipped his head in acknowledgement. "Okay, then. I'll say goodnight to you both."

With that, he opened the door, stepped out, and closed it firmly behind him. Immediately, her heart lamented its loss. Her brain tried to argue, but her emotions would have none of it.

Hazel cared deeply for the man. Her so-called threads had become intricately entwined with his, and there was no pretending otherwise.

Funny that she didn't seem to care so much anymore. They might have the world standing between them, but they'd figure it out.

CHAPTER SEVEN

In the backroom of her shop, Hazel pulled the tea strainer from her favorite mug. She sniffed the newly-created tea and closed her eyes with a relaxed smile.

Heavenly.

Inspired by the popularity of her iced teas at the May Day church event, she had decided to try crafting some different blends. Her first attempt to combine blueberries, pineapple, hibiscus and rooibos had turned out bland and watery.

So, she'd upped the amount of pineapple and let it steep for five minutes longer.

If the smell was any indication, this recipe would taste much better. She blew on the top of the liquid and took a tiny sip.

Yes. Very nice. She might be able to sell some of it during the winter months, but she'd specifically crafted this one to be enjoyed cold, a sweet refreshment on a hot summer day.

As soon as it cooled, she'd pour it over ice and take another taste.

In the meantime, she corrected the handwritten recipe in her book so that she'd remember exactly how she'd made it, including adjustments.

The phone sitting on the end of her workbench buzzed. She cast a sideways glance at it and smiled.

Peter.

Since the moment he'd walked out her door the night before, she'd been looking forward to seeing him again.

"Good morning." Happiness colored her words.

"Good morning, lovely witch."

She gasped at his greeting and glanced around even though she knew she was completely alone. Even if anyone had been there, they wouldn't have heard anyway. "Be careful with your words, sir."

Peter chuckled. "Don't worry. I'm standing outside your shop, and there's no one around to hear. They're all gathered at the opposite end of the street."

She drew her brows together and headed toward the shop's front door. Peter lifted his chin in greeting when he saw her, and she hung up the phone. She turned the lock on the door, and he pulled it open.

Before she could say anything, he had her in his arms with his mouth on hers. "Missed you."

She allowed her mind and senses to drift along in the lovely world he created with his kiss.

When he pulled back, she sighed with contentment.

She wouldn't mind starting all her days that way. "Could you do that every morning?"

He lifted his brows in surprise, and she realized he'd misunderstood her meaning.

"I didn't mean like first thing in the morning, like married or living together kind of stuff." She didn't dislike the idea, but she didn't want to scare the guy. "Just that it was really nice, and..."

He smiled and touched the center of her lips, sending sensual shivers careening through her. "It was really nice."

He gave her another quick kiss and then pointed his thumb over his shoulder. "I wouldn't mind standing here kissing you all day, but you're probably going to want to come and see this."

She glanced past him, toward the direction he'd indicated. A large group of people stood on the corner, all facing toward something in the middle. "What's going on?"

He took her hand and tugged her from the shop. "Come see."

Together, they walked toward the crowd. As they neared, she could hear someone spouting the evils of witchcraft, and she knew without a doubt the person was Timothy Franklin.

She squinted in annoyance and shook her head.

"This is a serious problem, folks," Timothy announced. "We can't become complacent. That's what we've done for the past five years, and look, they're coming out of the woodwork again like cockroaches."

Hazel opened her mouth the slightest and gaped at Peter. She mouthed, "Cockroaches?"

He gave a slight shrug.

June Porter raised her hand. "What are we going to do? We've lost our priest, so we can't exorcise them."

If it wasn't such a serious matter, Hazel would have laughed. Exorcisms only worked on demonic spirits. Most witches and wiccans were the furthest thing from that. If June had studied religion at all, she'd know that.

Rosalinda Valentine moved closer to Timothy and turned to face the group. She scanned the crowd with kind, deep brown eyes. Dark hair peppered with silver and a plump figure made her seem like a grandmother looking over her grandchildren.

"I have some news to share. The parish leader called me this morning and asked if I would return to my previous position at the church, and I told them yes."

Murmurs grew among the crowd, but most people seemed appreciative of her acceptance.

"Most of you are aware that I stepped down because of differences of opinion with Father Christopher." She held up a hand. "Don't get me wrong. I fully respected his position and mourn the loss of him like most in town. But if there's a way I can help transition his replacement so that we have help sooner, I'm happy to do so."

Timothy placed a hand on her shoulder. "Thank you, Rosalinda. We all appreciate what you've done for Stonebridge."

She turned a grateful smile in his direction. "The church is sending a temporary replacement. He should be here by Saturday. I'll fill him in on our troubles."

Sighs of relief rippled through the crowd.

Timothy nodded. "In the meantime, I've done some research on ways to combat witches who might try to infiltrate our town. For all we know, there may be some among us right now."

He glanced across the crowd. When his gaze landed on Hazel, she worked to give him her best impression of a relieved smile.

Rosalinda turned to Timothy. "Tell us what we can do."

"Holy water." He nodded to the crowd. "Past citizens of Stonebridge used it to identify witches. Sprinkle a little on a suspected person's skin. You should be able to tell right away."

"You've got to be kidding me," Peter muttered.

Hazel shushed him. Deep inside, she was smiling. Let them toss all the holy water they wanted.

Timothy pushed his glasses further up his nose. "If you think you or your family might be afflicted, contact me, and I can supply you with as much as you need. As we speak, a priest friend of mine is blessing gallons of water for this serious outbreak. I have a few containers here with me today."

Neighbors glanced around and nodded at each other.

Hazel wanted to drop her face into her palm and laugh at their naivety but couldn't.

Peter tugged her back from the crowd. "Let's go."

Mrs. Lemon glanced up at them with rheumy eyes as they passed. "Don't forget to take some holy water."

Peter placed a friendly hand on her shoulder. "I'll let you all go first and wait until Timothy gets more from his friend. I'm better equipped to take care of myself and worry more about all of you."

Mrs. Lemon nodded with a solemn gaze. "Just remember, bullets can't stop curses."

He gave her a gentle smile. "Don't worry. I won't wait long to snag some for me and Hazel, too."

Her weathered lips turned into a genuine smile. "You're a good man, Chief Parrish."

They both wished the older woman well and headed back to Hazel's shop. She left the door unlocked behind them since she'd be opening soon anyway.

Irritation rolled off Peter like white-capped waves hitting shore, but he waited until they were safely in the teashop before he spoke. "Looks like my men and I will have our hands full trying to keep unreasonable fear from turning into all-out frenzy."

She gestured for him to follow her into the backroom. "That scares me more than I want to admit, but if all they're doing is using holy water as a litmus test, we have nothing to worry about."

She faced him and took both of his hands. "Do you want to know what's funny about all this? Timothy comes from a long line of witches. He belongs to one of the originals, the Named."

Peter's features twisted into amused disbelief. "Are you sure? He's one of the biggest proponents against witchcraft in this town."

"Right?" She snorted. "It would serve him right if someone doused him with holy water, and he shriveled up like a raisin."

He chuckled. "Now, there's a visual I can appreciate."

His gaze grew serious, and he squeezed her hands. "Can I ask how you learned about Timothy's heritage?"

The forever battle that raged inside her intensified again. She wished desperately that she could tell him everything. "A friend. I can't say who."

A cloak of sadness fell over his beautiful green eyes, and she hated herself for causing it.

"I'm sorry, Peter." She had to find a way to fix this. "Give me a little more time, okay? I've barely earned the trust of this person, and I don't want to ruin it."

"What about our trust?"

She shrugged and sent him a hopeful look. "It's there. Just have a little faith."

He didn't argue, but she could tell he didn't fully accept her answer, either.

She moved to the cooled cup of tea she'd brewed earlier. "Hey, want to try my new iced tea?"

He hesitated and then, by degrees, let go of his impatience. "Is it any good?"

She scoffed. "I should hope so." Really, though.

"What's it called?"

"I haven't decided yet." She pulled an ice cube tray from the freezer and filled two plastic cups. "Maybe you can help me. Pineapple and blueberries are the main ingredients, mixed with a red bush herbal tea."

A sly grin crossed his lips. "What about Pineberry Bush Tea?"

She almost said no, but then paused, rolling the words through her mind a few times. "Actually, I kind of like it. Pineberry Bush Tea. Sounds very holistic."

He gave her a dubious look. "Don't tell me it's holistic. It's a big turn off."

She laughed and poured the red tea over the ice, loving the way it crackled. "Do you even know what holistic means?"

"Disgusting." Then he smiled, giving away the fact that he teased her.

She handed a cup to him. "Natural, holistic things are good for you."

He glanced at the tea. "Not all of them."

"This one is. Try it." She lifted her cup and waited for him to do the same. Then they drank together.

Full flavors burst on her tongue, and she knew she had a winner. He smiled, confirming her conclusion. "This is really good."

She nodded with excitement. "It really is. I have to say, I'm kind of proud of it."

He took another drink, and then smacked his lips. "You should be."

"Oh, hey. I have an idea. I should make it with holy water and watch it fly off the shelves."

Peter lifted his cup in a toast. "Do it, and you'll be rich."

He widened his eyes as his emotions turned serious, putting her on alert. "I can't believe I forgot the biggest reason I'd come to see you this morning. Tests are back. Your tea tested negative for any toxins, peanut or otherwise."

Her breath whooshed out of her in relief. "I mean, I knew it would because I didn't poison him. But then you hear stuff on the news all the time about people who were wrongly accused and suffered for it."

He wrapped a possessive arm around her waist and tugged her to him. "That's part of the reason I sent the evidence to a neighboring, impartial lab. I didn't want to chance any tampering. With things turning crazy, who knows what might be going through people's heads. Some want the truth. Others want a scapegoat."

She stood on tiptoe, pressing her face against the hollow below his ear. His scent infused her, and she kissed his neck. "I'll say it again. Thank you for watching out for me."

He cupped her chin and tilted her face toward him, pressing a warm kiss on her lips. "I wish I had the same good news for Lucy."

CHAPTER EIGHT

N
o, Peter. Don't tell me that Lucy murdered Father Christopher."

His original news had left Hazel relieved and buoyant one moment but now heartbroken. "I can't believe that dear woman could take a life. She was so good to help out Cora after Belinda died."

To Hazel, Lobster Lucy was one of those people who had a heart big enough for everyone.

"I'm not saying she did it, Hazel, but it doesn't look good for her." He drew a rough finger down her cheek as he studied her eyes. "That's where we'll focus our investigation for now. Thank God you've been cleared, which allows me to take over again, so things don't get out of hand."

Yes, that was a good thing on both accounts. "I'm sure John won't like to have his power usurped so soon. I'm also very glad he's no longer in control. The person in charge of protecting the town needs to have unbiased opinions. At least as much as possible."

"He was never fully in charge. Just over this one investigation. But, you're right, he's not happy. He'll be even less happy after we discuss his career this afternoon."

She liked the sound of that. "Are you going to fire him?"

"I wish I could, but, technically, he didn't do anything wrong."

"Are you kidding me? Between him and Timothy, Stonebridge is likely to have an all-out civil war." Someone had to stop those crazy fools.

He disagreed with a shake of his head. "You can't have a civil war if you don't know who you're fighting, can you? Timothy and John are taking pot shots in the dark. For now, they're clueless."

She stepped back and folded her arms. "You hope."

He lifted a shoulder and let it drop. "One can never know for sure, but I keep a close eye on everyone and my ears open. You know, it might help if I knew who was on the opposite side. I could pay special attention to them which would help me keep them safer."

She sighed. Too many of their discussions led back to this point. "I promise, Peter, I don't know who they all are. Belinda was a witch. So was Glenys, but you already know those two. Timothy denies his heritage, and then one other person. That could be it for all I know."

"It's Cora, isn't it?"

She clamped her lips tight and narrowed her gaze. "Don't ask me. I can't tell you."

He nodded thoughtfully.

Maybe he had figured it out, but she wouldn't confirm anything. "Perhaps there isn't anyone else in town," she added.

He tugged a hand free from her folded arms and twined his fingers with hers. "Is that what you believe?"

She thought for a moment and then shook her head. "I've heard there's a coven in town. That makes me think there must be at least a handful more. My friend told me something interesting about another curse. She said the original witches cast a spell that would keep Stonebridge from ever being free from witches. A descendant from each of their lines would always be drawn to town. If one left or died, another would take his or her place."

He snorted. "Great. We'll always enjoy the perks of civil unrest."

She cast him a sideways grin. "Unless the town learns to accept witches and treat them decent."

"Glenys was far from decent. Some of the stuff she tried that day..." He shook his head as though to erase the memory.

"Yes, well, neither was Mr. Winthrop or Timothy Franklin. Or sadly, even John Bartles."

Peter made a face as he scratched the side of his chin. "I have to admit that one really shocked me. When you gave me that Sons of Stonebridge document..." He shook his head in disappointment.

"Same. But I guess it's better to know your enemies." She turned to face him and pinned him against the counter with her body. "What I want to know is what you're going to do to help poor Lucy."

He chuckled. "I'm surprised you haven't already started your own investigation."

The idea did appeal to her, but... "You're always telling me to stay out of official police business, and I think I finally learned that lesson with Glenys. My involvement there could have cost me everything. My friends, my life, you. If I haven't said it before, thank you for not condemning me."

He tightened his arms about her waist. "I never would have condemned you."

"But you told me witches have no place in Stonebridge."

"Why would a person want to be where they're not wanted? It only creates more chaos and heartache for everyone involved."

She sent him an understanding smile. "But why should we have to be the ones to leave? It was our ancestors' town back then just as much as the others. Stonebridge is a beautiful place. I can see why they wouldn't want to go."

He tilted his head to the side. "Point well-taken."

The bell on the outer door chimed, signaling a customer. She smiled. "Possible first sale of the day. Gotta love that."

He chuckled and released her. "Yep, gotta love it. I need to get back to work, too. After yesterday, we have our hands busy."

Very true. "You work too hard. You make sure you take care of yourself. Don't forget to eat."

He grinned. "I wouldn't mind if you invited me to your place for dinner one day this week."

"Ah... I see. Playing my concern against me. Good thing I have a soft heart."

"I love your heart."

The center of her soul squeezed with happiness. "Sweet talking will get you everywhere. I'm eating at Cora's tonight, but I'll let you know if tomorrow or Wednesday works."

He kissed her on the cheek. "Sounds wonderful."

Together, they walked into the outer area where Hazel found Rosalinda studying the canisters of tea sitting on the counter.

Rosalinda wasn't one of her regular customers, but she liked her. She'd stop by every other week or so. Hazel always enjoyed her sunny disposition and glowing aura. Not to mention the sales.

Peter tipped his head in greeting. "Morning, Rosalinda."

She looked up with a bright smile. "Good morning, Chief."

Peter placed a quick kiss on Hazel's cheek and headed out the door.

Rosalinda grinned with mischief. "I'm so glad you two found each other. After his wife died, we all were so heartbroken for him."

Hazel nodded in sympathy. "I can't imagine how devastating it must have been. Did you know his wife well?"

She tilted her head from side to side, causing her salt and pepper hair to sway. "Not really. Sarah didn't come to church often, but she liked to join the ladies' quilting group. A pleasant, kind person. Such a tragedy."

That was putting it mildly. "Peter said it was a hit-and-run accident."

Rosalinda's eyes widened. "That's the official word."

Questions popped into her head left and right, and she fought to dismiss them. She'd promised herself to turn over a new leaf and search for peace in life, not the drama that came from solving crimes.

She managed to hold off for two seconds before she thought she might die from curiosity. "You make it sound like there's an unofficial version of what happened."

Rosalinda slid a blue ceramic teapot toward Hazel, indicating she wanted to purchase it. "There have been rumors."

"What kind?" she asked without hesitating at all this time.

She studied Hazel's eyes for a long moment as though deciding whether she should trust her. "I'm not sure you're aware, but I used to work for the church as its secretary."

"I heard that outside a few moments ago. They've called you to come back."

She nodded. "One day," she said carefully. "I was walking toward Father Christopher's office, and I heard him on the phone with someone. It was right after Peter's wife died. The Father asked if 'she' was dead and then said good."

Hazel's jaw dropped. "Was he talking about Sarah?"

Rosalinda shrugged. "I don't know."

The older lady crossed herself. "He was not a good man, Hazel. I would never want to see anyone die, but I'm glad he's no longer leading our church."

"Me, too. That's very disturbing to hear."

"I asked him about it afterward, but he said he was talking about a deceased person in another town, and when he'd said 'good', he'd meant he was glad to hear the services went well."

"But you don't believe that was true."

She shook her head. "Shortly after that, things escalated between us, donations went missing, and he asked the church to replace me."

Now, Hazel understood why she'd gotten such a negative vibe from the priest. She'd learned not to ignore her senses, but that didn't mean she could completely avoid awful people, especially not when being near him had helped to protect her own secrets.

Rosalinda expelled a breath and smiled. "Let's forget about that nasty business. It's in the past. I, for one, am ready to look forward to the future."

"That sounds like a good choice."

Rosalinda lifted her purse and set it on the counter. "The reason I'm here today is that I would like to purchase a teapot for the church and request a delivery of a large canister of your youth tea, the one with currants and apples that gives an old lady like me a spring to her step. Every two weeks, if you please. If I'm going to be working full time, I'm going to treat myself. A cup of your tea always brightens my mornings. Sometimes, I even have two."

Hazel smiled with delight. "Of course. But I might suggest smaller canisters every week instead the larger one. Same price, and your tea will be fresher."

Rosalinda lifted interested brows. "Is that so? All this time, I've been buying bigger canisters because I thought I'd save money. But, you're right, the first cup out of the canister is always the best."

Hazel pulled the book containing her delivery customers from under the counter and opened it. "Let's see. I deliver that way every Tuesday. I could start tomorrow and would be there around eleven. Does that work for you?"

She clapped her hands together. "That would be perfect. Before I leave, I'm also going to sample a cup of Happy Day, if that's okay."

Hazel waved away her concern. "It's always okay. That's what I have my sampling station set up for." She paused. "Hey, would you like to try something new I've been working on? I'm calling it Pineberry Bush Tea. It's best served iced."

"Sounds like fun. I'd love to."

"Great. I'll be right back."

Hazel headed into her workroom, her mind buzzing with thoughts. Maybe she'd stand on the street corner and hand out samples of tea like Timothy had handed out hatred. That might encourage more business and good feelings toward mankind.

Also, she needed to figure out a way to ask Peter more details about his wife's death without making it seem like she was meddling again. But she'd be remiss to not tell him what she'd learned. She'd just have to make sure he understood that Rosalinda had offered the information, and she hadn't gone looking for it.

CHAPTER NINE

Hazel locked up the teashop just after seven that evening and headed down the cobblestone sidewalk toward Cora's. Up until now, the twinkling white lights strung up in the trees had been turned off since Christmas, but the town had relit them to add ambience to the upcoming summer season. Strolling down the sidewalk with tiny white lights glowing overhead like stars as a soft balmy breeze caressed her skin soothed her soul and erased all stresses of the day.

This was why witches stayed in Stonebridge. Despite its turbulence, the town carried a deep abiding peace in its soil and trees, and that intangible gift soaked into people's souls whether they realized it or not.

The curse of being Clarabelle's offspring might have been what brought her here, but this was why she stayed. With all this beauty, it was hard to see living in Stonebridge as a curse.

Halfway down the block, an unwelcome anomaly screeched across her serenity like a needle on a vinyl record. She halted in her tracks, searching for the source, as familiar angst and heartbreak surrounded her.

She surveyed the area and then spotted him standing across the street watching her. She closed her eyes and launched a desperate prayer to the Blessed Mother to save her.

When she lifted her lids, she found Victor Black strutting across the street like he owned it. Taut muscles stretched with each step, and confidence radiated like it should from one of the most powerful witches along the eastern seaboard.

He stepped onto the sidewalk next to her, ice blue eyes devouring her in an instant. "Hazel."

She gritted her teeth as anger boiled inside. "What in the Samhain are you doing here?"

He raked a hand through long, dark bangs, pushing them over top of his head. "Your mother sent me."

Disbelief exploded inside her. *"Say that again."*

That woman might have birthed her, but Hazel wasn't above hexing or disowning her.

One side of his mouth tilted upward in the sexy grin that used to leave her weak in the knees. "Your mom. She was worried that she hadn't heard from you."

Seriously? She couldn't believe she'd spaced her weekly email letting her know she was fine. "I missed one stupid email. She didn't need to call in the cavalry."

"Cavalry, huh?" He nodded at what he perceived was a compliment. "And it's been two weeks since you've emailed, not one."

She clenched her fists. Out of all the people her mother could have sent, she'd picked the worst. She knew her mom hadn't wanted her to break up with Victor, but Hazel had also avoided telling her all the ugly details.

"She could have called."

He shrugged, and she wished she could wipe the cocky smile off his face. Maybe Clarabelle's book had a spell for that.

"You know how she worries. I think she wanted firsthand knowledge that everything was well with you."

She pointed an angry finger at him. "First off, asking *you* to see to my well-being is laughable, and second, I'm a grown woman capable of taking care of myself without having my mother check on me every two seconds."

He shook his head, his expression suggesting she was overreacting. "Come on, Hazel. You know I cared about you. I still do." He placed a hand over his heart. "Deeply."

"No." She shook her head vehemently. "No, no, no and no! You lied to me, and you cheated on me."

"I didn't lie. I just didn't tell you everything. I didn't want to hurt you."

She couldn't believe her ears. *"You were with another woman."*

He reached for her, but she stepped back and held out her palms toward him. "There were no feelings involved," he said.

She stared in stunned disbelief for several long seconds and then inhaled a deep, fortifying breath. "Get out of my life and out of my town. Now."

His eyes pleaded with her. "Hazel... Be reasonable."

"Now." She pointed south down Main Street. "Get on whatever broom you rode here on and disappear from my life forever."

"It's a Harley," he said with a grin.

She growled and shook her head. "Leave. Just leave." She turned and marched toward Cora's without giving him a backward glance.

Hazel jerked open the door of Cora's Café still fuming. She didn't know if she was angrier at her mother or Victor.

She glanced about the café but didn't spot Cora.

Bertie, Cora's new server, greeted her with a warm smile. The older, sturdier lady might not provide the customers with the same eye candy as Belinda had, but she doubted she'd take advantage of senile old men, either.

"Hey, Bertie. Have you seen Cora? I'm supposed to meet her here."

Bertie tucked a pencil behind her ear. "She stepped out to drop off an order two doors down. Told me to tell you she'd be right back. Why don't you take a seat, and I'll bring you a drink?"

Hazel smiled and allowed the woman's friendly attitude to erase some of her anger. Not all people in the world were obnoxious like her mother or jerks like Victor.

"That would be lovely. I'll take ice water, please." That might help cool off her insides as well.

Bertie dropped off her water. Hazel lifted the glass to drink and spotted Lachlan, her favorite person from the bank, walking through the door. He glanced about, met her gaze, and headed in her direction with a friendly smile.

Beautiful blue eyes peered at her through dark glasses. "Hey, Hazel. Have you seen Cora?"

She checked her watch, noting that ten minutes had passed already. "She's missing in action. I'm waiting for her, too." She opened her hand to invite him to sit.

He slid onto the opposite side of the booth. "That's right. She said you were coming here to have dinner with her."

Hazel lifted her brow. "You and Cora seem to get along well."

He smiled and nodded. "We have some great conversations."

Only conversations? Hazel hoped it might turn into something more. "Heard anything on my loan for the house on Hemlock yet?"

He narrowed his eyes in thought. "Uh...I think it's in process. Everything is a disaster. The bank ran so smoothly when Glenys was in charge, but now that she's gone, auditors have discovered missing money, fake accounts and all kinds of weird stuff they hadn't noticed before. We're working to get things back in order."

Magic, Hazel assumed. Glenys had probably used what she had to work things in her favor.

Feminine laughter drew their attention to the front door, and Cora walked in with Victor right behind her. Cora's cheeks were flushed, and Hazel was sure she'd missed the predatory look in Victor's eyes. "You are the biggest flirt I've ever met."

Victor glanced over Cora's head and sent Hazel a crafty smile.

Deep anger rumbled like a volcano. If he thought flirting with Cora would make her jealous, he'd have to think again. She turned her attention to Lachlan who also watched the public display with irritation and suspicion shining from his gaze.

"Who's that?" he asked Hazel without taking his eyes off Cora.

Her sigh was heavy enough that it drew his attention. "That would be my ex-boyfriend. My mother sent him from Boston to check on me."

His look hardened. "He needs to get out of Dodge. Today."

"That's exactly what I told him."

More laughter and teasing drifted their way, fueling Lachlan's anger until Hazel feared he would combust. She cursed her bad luck and stood. "Will you excuse me?"

He grunted in answer but didn't take his gaze off the flirting couple.

She strode up to them, and Cora turned to her with a smile.

Hazel shook her head in answer. "This man that you're flirting with is one of the worst scoundrels this side of England. I'd suggest you run as far as you can."

Cora's expression turned shocked.

Hazel didn't wait for her reply but gripped Victor's forearm as hard as she could and pulled the leech away from her best friend. "We're leaving."

Victor grinned. "Bye, Cora. I'll catch you later." He walked happily alongside Hazel until they were outside.

She rounded on him. "What do you think you're doing?"

He shrugged. "Chance meeting between me and Cora. I'd just gotten on my bike when she walked by. *She* seemed appreciative of what I have to offer, so I asked her if she'd like a ride."

"And she said yes?" Was her friend insane?

"It was only a little trip around the block, but I didn't mind having her—"

"Stop!" Hazel yelled over his words. "I don't want to hear what you thought, and I never want to hear you talk about or see my best friend again."

He flashed the dangerous smile that she'd once thought so attractive. "Best friends, huh? Maybe we could—"

"You disgust me, and you need to leave."

He turned his palms upward and shrugged. "Can't. Not until I'm sure you're okay."

She gestured to her body with a dramatic sweep of her hands. "I'm standing right here in front of you. I'm obviously okay."

He raked the hair off his forehead. "Yeah, but there is that little issue about those in town who might hurt you and some of the other witches. I can't report to your mother until I know you're safe."

He knew far too much for being in town such a short time. "How did you hear about that?"

"Let's see." He turned his gaze skyward. "The police had you in custody when I first arrived, questioning you about a murder. Uh...there's a maniacal dude who works at the library who thinks he can wipe out our kind. Do you want me to continue?"

"Wait," he said before she could give him a piece of her mind. "You're also dating the police chief. Is that right?"

She pasted on a pretty smile. "That's right. I am. And he treats me much better than you ever did." She sensed her barb hitting home and took pleasure in it.

Victor narrowed his gaze, and Hazel relished the irritation building in him. He never had been able to hide his feelings from her. "Does he have powers?"

She wasn't about to let Victor downplay Peter's value. "He can kiss better than anyone I know."

The darkness surrounding him grew to a point that left her anxious, and she decided to cull the insults. The last thing she wanted was an angry, jealous man on her hands who was highly skilled with magic.

He curled his lips back into a dangerous smile. "I was referring to his abilities as a witch."

She met his gaze directly. "No magic."

The intense air around them settled. "And you're happy with that?"

"Victor, what do you want? It's obvious I'm fine. I have friends here, including witches, that look out for me. I don't need you to protect me."

"He's not going to make you happy like I can."

He'd already exceeded Victor by far. "That's not true because you and I will never be together again."

He nodded, a sly smile curving his lips. "I'm still going to hang around town for a couple of days, just to be sure. If I head back now, your mom won't believe me, and then she'll send someone worse."

As if she could. Still, she knew a losing battle when she saw one and refused to allow him to keep her sucked in any longer. Indifference would be her constant companion until Victor left. "Whatever. Just stay out of my way and leave my best friend alone."

CHAPTER TEN

Hazel's thoughts tortured her the entire night. By the time morning arrived, she struggled to make her brain work, but she was grateful she didn't have to try to sleep any longer.

Was Victor outside her house?

Should she tell Peter about him or hope that he'd leave before Peter discovered his existence?

Then again Peter knew everything about this town. She'd have to explain her former relationship with Victor, but how exactly did she do that?

Was she delusional to think she could have a relationship with a regular guy in a town like this?

Round and around her thoughts went. If she didn't stop, her head would likely explode.

She arrived at work early. Packed her deliveries for the day, and then tried to decide on another iced tea she might like to try, but her creative brain cells were non-existent, probably still back in her room snoozing.

Gretta arrived at work on time, looking as perky as ever with a crisp white blouse and an enviable handbag the color of watermelon. "Looks like you're already ready to go."

"Yep," Hazel answered as she pulled her phone from below the counter and tucked it in her pocket. She turned to face Gretta, and a flash of green dropped from Gretta's hand onto the floor below. A splooshing sound registered milliseconds before water sprinkled onto her toes and sandals, and she discovered a deflated green balloon resting near her feet.

She lifted her gaze to Gretta. "What the heck?"

"Oh, sorry. It slipped."

Her assistant was the worst liar ever, given away by the purple that surrounded the yellow in her aura. Hazel widened her eyes. "It slipped?"

Gretta nodded.

She had no time or patience for nonsense this morning. "It didn't slip, Gretta. Tell me why you're dropping a water balloon on my feet."

She hesitated, looking guiltier than sin. "It was slippery."

Hazel dropped her head into her hand and sighed. Things in Stonebridge were getting out of hand. She met Gretta's gaze straight on. "Did there happen to be holy water in that balloon?"

Gretta's expression fell. "I'm so sorry, Hazel. Timothy has everyone spooked, and some kids were selling these out in front of the library. I decided to be safe and buy one for all the people I hang out with. You can't be too careful, you know?" She opened her bag to show Hazel a large stash of colorful balloons.

She couldn't bring herself to berate Gretta for something she didn't understand. "Well, now that it's obvious I'm not Satan's spawn, would you mind grabbing some paper towels from the back, so I can wipe my feet? I'll let *you* clean up the mess on the floor."

"Of course. I'm so sorry." She hurried into the back room and came out with a wad of paper towels. She shoved some at Hazel. "I feel like an idiot now."

Hazel shook her head and tried to pretend everything was cool. "Maybe I should stop and get some balloons myself."

Gretta nodded encouragingly before she knelt to wipe water. "You probably should. Those kids are making bank, but it helps us all."

She might do that after all. Her purchase would look good to the residents. She could throw them at the jerks in town and still seem perfectly reasonable.

Perhaps they'd give her a discount for a bulk purchase, and she could use them to chase Victor out of town. He hated getting wet once he was dressed.

Hazel wiped her toes, tossed the towels, and scooped up her packages. "If you could spread the word that you tested me and I'm fine, I'd appreciate it. The last thing I need is to be pelted by others."

Gretta gave her a sheepish grin. "I'll be sure to do that."

"Thanks." Hazel left the shop hoping the rest of her day would be better than the first.

Pedaling around Stonebridge in the morning sunshine refreshed her much more than her restless night's sleep. By the time she dropped off four deliveries and then stopped at the old church, she was a new woman. She might run out of steam long before bedtime, but she was good for now.

She parked her bike, lifted her last package, and headed for the church's rough-hewn wooden doors. The one she tugged on opened without a squeak. She stepped inside and discovered absolute quiet, marred only by the loud thumping of her heart.

She'd never been particularly bothered by churches before. To each his own, she believed. But the hatred in this town that had soaked into the walls of the church years ago, still clung to the atmosphere today. She was sure the Sons of Stonebridge encouraged it.

The doors to the chapel were open, and she walked closer, peering inside. Pews were encased in rich-looking wooden boxes that separated them from others. Arched windows filled the room with sunshine that sent shards of light raining from the massive chandelier. The history that resided in the building amazed her.

Growing up, she'd loved learning about the patriots who had inhabited the same land she walked on, and she knew not all those people hated witches. Most probably didn't pay them much mind, if they even believed they existed.

But the ones who did harbor ill will toward witches had sure caused much tragedy.

Footsteps behind her drew her attention, and she turned.

The mild-mannered church secretary smiled in greeting. "Hazel. Welcome." Rosalinda walked forward with outstretched hands.

Hazel took them and squeezed, sending love and light to her friend. "This is a magnificent building. So much history."

Rosalinda glanced about the chapel and nodded. "I always did love working here. At times, I could find the most amazing peace. Especially when the Father was out."

There was obviously no love lost between Rosalinda and Father Christopher.

She met Hazel's gaze and grinned. "Come in my office so I can pay you."

Hazel walked reverently across the polished wooden floors. Impressions of many people bumped against her, so much that she eventually blocked them out.

Rosalinda led her into a section of the church that had been added on during later years, and then into a small, sparsely furnished but well-organized office. "Have a seat. This will just take me a second." She opened a bottom drawer and pulled out her wallet.

Hazel glanced about while Rosalinda retrieved her money. The sight of Lucy's name on a handwritten list on the desk caught her attention. Dan Cullpepper. Mayor Elwood, Lucy—

Rosalinda slipped the paper off her desk before she could continue reading and into a drawer. Hazel's cheeks heated with embarrassment, but at least Rosalinda hadn't commented on Hazel's rudeness.

"I could send you a monthly bill if you like," Hazel offered, trying to pretend the last thirty seconds hadn't happened.

Rosalinda gave her a gentle smile, and Hazel felt no anger or hostility for being nosy. "No, I don't mind paying each week. It will give us a chance to chat."

Hazel wasn't surprised. Wanting to visit when she dropped off deliveries seemed to be a common thread among most of her clients.

Hazel knew she'd been gifted with the ability to sense others' emotions better than most. She'd often been told she had a calming, empathetic presence, so it made sense people wanted to talk to someone who understood them.

Hazel shrugged, pretending that darned piece of paper Rosalinda had slid into the drawer wasn't calling her name. "Then that works well for me, too. I love getting out and meeting the community."

Rosalinda slid the money across the desk and gave her a warm smile. "You've been here only a few months, but you've fit right in, and we love having you. We can't say that about everyone."

Hazel chuckled. "Well, if it helps you to know, Gretta doused me with holy water this morning just to be sure I was safe to be around."

Rosalinda gasped, but Hazel sensed laughter along with it. "She didn't."

"Oh, yeah. She did." Hazel gave a good show of resigned acceptance. "Dropped a water balloon right on my bare toes. If I'd have known what she was up to, I would have dropped to my knees or screamed to scare her."

Rosalinda didn't laugh like Hazel thought she would. "That would be funny, but I wouldn't mess around with stuff like this. I've been in Stonebridge long enough to see people go crazy."

The woman was certainly old enough to have witnessed plenty. "Were you here, then, during the last May Day death?"

"Sure was," Rosalinda replied. "I'd been married maybe a year when it happened. The whole town was on edge with accusations flying left and right."

Hazel's brain flooded with thoughts. "Timothy isn't old enough to remember, is he?"

"No. He wouldn't have been born yet."

Hazel reminded herself to tread carefully when talking about Timothy to Rosalinda. "You two seem to be good friends."

The older woman's gaze turned thoughtful. "Hmm... I wouldn't say good friends. Friendly, for sure. He comes to church a lot, so I've gotten to know him somewhat. Nice enough man when he keeps his paranoia under control."

Hazel gave her a sympathetic nod. "It's hard when we live in fear of witches nesting in our town." She might as well start using their lingo.

"Very true, young lady. We need to protect our own." Rosalinda dropped her wallet back in the drawer and closed it. "Your cute man was here a while ago."

"Here?" Peter had said he didn't have much use for church after his wife died. "Just to pay a visit?"

Rosalinda gave her a conspiratorial smile. "No. He was asking questions about anyone who might have had issues with Father Christopher."

She should act uninterested, thank Rosalinda for her order, and be on her way. But the curiosity bubbling inside her kept her firmly planted where she was. "Did you mention anyone?"

"I told him what I could. Poor Lucy doesn't deserve to take the fall for this, when it could have been so many other people. People who would have had an opportunity to mess with Lucy's strawberry tart."

"So, you're thinking that it would have made an easy target? I mean, Lucy had been bragging for days about presenting Father Christopher with a deliciously large strawberry tart."

Rosalinda nodded. "I would say it's highly possible, and I told Peter the same thing. Really, though, I think it might be the May Day Curse, and no one is guilty."

Then the woman's expression dropped, and she blinked rapidly. "I'm an awful person, Hazel. I'm so grateful he's no longer with us. I wish I would have done something about Father Christopher a long time ago. I kept my mouth shut about church matters but maybe I shouldn't have."

The outpouring of regret surprised Hazel. She reached across the desk and covered the poor woman's hand. "I'm sure you did the best you could and what you thought was right at that moment. Hindsight is a wonderful thing, but, unfortunately, it's not available to us in advance."

"They should choose you as the new priest. You're one of the most compassionate, understanding people I've met in my lifetime. Having someone like you to lead us would do wonders for this town."

Hazel laughed at the absurdity. "I'm not so sure about that. Besides, I have a hard time finding God's spirit inside the walls of a church."

Rosalinda widened her eyes as though Hazel had just told her a juicy secret. "Be careful who you say those words to. Some might misunderstand your meaning."

Hazel was well aware of that fact. "Yes, I know. Before all this happened, Lucy had invited Cora and me to attend church with her, and I'd considered it. Maybe I will again once everything settles down."

She couldn't ever see that happening, not unless she was forced to attend to save her reputation.

"Well," Rosalinda said with a kind smile. "You've been doused and passed with flying colors, so you'll be fine for now. We'll worry about your soul later."

Hazel tucked the money Rosalinda had given her into her shoulder bag and stood. "Thanks again for your regular order. I'll see you next week, if not sooner around town."

"I look forward to it. I can tell already that we're going to be very good friends."

Hazel wished she could say she felt the same, but it was impossible to truly let someone see her heart when she knew they wouldn't approve.

CHAPTER ELEVEN

Peter had suggested dinner at her house one night that week, but Hazel decided burgers on the fly for lunch was a much better idea since she could no longer wait to talk to him.

She checked with Margaret to ensure Peter was in the office and hadn't eaten yet. After that, she followed up with a phone call to Gretta informing her she'd be in later, and then she headed to Cora's.

Hazel placed her order with Bertie and then searched out her friend and found her in the storage room taking inventory.

Cora glanced up and smiled. "Hey, lady. What are you doing here? And more importantly, what happened with that cute guy last night?"

She gave Cora a look that suggested she might have lost some brain cells. "Didn't you hear what I said to you then?"

Cora looked at her the same way. "You spouted some nonsense about a scoundrel in England. Who even uses that word? Then you grabbed his arm and took off. I should remind you that you're the one who needs to be careful since you already have a boyfriend."

Hazel stared at her in shock for a moment and then started laughing. "Oh, Blessed Mother. He hexed you."

"What?" Denial scattered around them like marbles dropping to the floor. "No, he didn't."

Hazel held her gaze and gave her several slow emphatic nods. "Did he mention he's a witch? Did he mention he's one of the most powerful male witches around?"

Hazel's voice turned snarky. "Also, did he mention that he used to be my boyfriend until he cheated on me?"

Cora blinked several times, and her eyes grew clearer. "What a creep." She paused and then nodded. "I think the jerk did put a hex on me. I can feel it."

Hazel gave a sarcastic laugh. "He's good, and when I say good, I mean trouble."

Cora lifted a hand and let it drop in defeat. "I can't believe I didn't see that coming. I should have known he was too good to be true."

"I hear ya, girlfriend. Just be glad you didn't fall in love before you found out what he was, and he broke your heart."

She huffed, sounding disappointed. "No kidding. Why is he here anyway? Did he come searching for you?"

Hazel rolled her eyes, still angry. "My beloved, loyal mother, of all people, sent him here to check on me."

Cora tucked in her lips as though she was repressing a grin. "Ouch. There didn't seem to be any love lost between you two last night."

Hazel shook her head repeatedly. "Oh, he'd get back together in an instant if I'd agree. Just so long as I don't mind other women, which shouldn't matter because his relationships with them would all be purely physical with no feelings involved. According to him, that is."

"Wow. He's a real piece of work. Which is a shame because he's hotter than hot."

"I don't want to hear it. I don't want to hear another word about him, and I hope I never see him again."

Cora's expression grew dreamy. "Such a waste of perfectly good man-flesh."

"Man-flesh?" She snorted. "Please. You wouldn't want a delicious-looking, sugar and cinnamon sprinkled cream puff if it was filled with rotting fish from the docks."

She wrinkled her nose in fake disappointment. "I could still lick the outside."

Hazel laughed at her tenacity. "No wonder we women are always finding ourselves in trouble with the wrong man."

"It's true," Cora agreed. "We fall for the delicious outside every time. Speaking of hot guys, what's up with yours? I can't imagine he's happy about..."

"Victor. I'm sure he wouldn't be, but I haven't told him yet."

"Oh, sugar, you had better not wait on that. A hot ex in town can be hard on a budding relationship."

Budding? She wanted to remind Cora she was the one who'd said their threads were already deeply intertwined. Instead, she sighed. "I'm actually headed there now. I figured I'd soften him up with a hamburger."

"Should have gone for the roast beef sandwich."

Hazel groaned. "Didn't think of that. Well, it can be my back up plan for later if this doesn't work. I wanted to ask him about the murder investigation, too. I was just at the church talking with Rosalinda, and it made me curious."

"I thought you were staying away from all that stuff."

She blinked away from Cora's discerning gaze. "Me, too, but it's impossible to not think about everything."

Cora snickered. "Yeah, I figured you wouldn't last long."

She wanted to argue that she wasn't *that* predictable, but she probably was. "Let me ask you first, since you know Lucy pretty well."

"I'll tell you right off the bat before you ask anything about her, she's helped me out numerous times. She has a heart of gold, and she's not a murderer."

Hazel hated to think the worst of her, too. "I know she's a wonderful person, and I feel terrible about the position she's in. Half the town is against her, and the other half doesn't believe she's capable of murder. I know she had trouble with Father Christopher and that it had something to do with marital counseling, but I have no idea what happened."

Cora set her clipboard down and dropped her pencil on top of it. "Let's go sit on the bench outside. I need some fresh air."

They wound their way through the café and out the front door where they both claimed spots on a nearby bench. The scent of fresh dirt and petunias encircled Hazel, and she inhaled until her lungs were full. A few cars drove by and a couple of tourists walked the cobblestone sidewalks, but not enough to disturb their privacy.

Cora bent her knee and slid it onto the bench between them as she turned to Hazel. "I'll be honest. Lucy is a tough lady. She's had to be. The pond scum she married, a deck hand on one of the commercial fishing boats, was a mean son of a gun. He drank too much, and when he did, he got physical."

Hazel's heart cracked. "Oh, no." She'd endured her fair share of emotional abuse in her lifetime, but nothing physical.

A dismal look blanched Cora's features. "Yeah, it got ugly. I think the only thing that allowed her to hold on that long was that he'd be gone for weeks. She'd threatened to kick him out numerous times, but he'd always convince her to keep him."

"Poor Lucy. And now this after she finally found peace."

Cora's gaze followed a car as it drove past. "I thought about putting a curse on him a few times, but Karma can be a beast when she wants. So, I steered clear and tried to be as much support as I could."

Hazel nodded. "Sometimes, that's all you can do."

Cora's focus grew distant. "The day he broke her arm, though, that was the day he broke her. He pleaded and pleaded to be forgiven, even promised to go to counseling. She finally agreed."

Hazel closed her eyes as a wave of disgust rolled over her. "And Father Christopher was who they sought for help."

"Yep," Cora said with finality. "Week after week they went to see him. At first, Lucy seemed very hopeful. She said Ed was trying, but that didn't last long. Then he was back to hitting her. Still, Father Christopher convinced her that if she left her husband without giving her marriage everything she had, which apparently included her life, then she'd go to hell."

"And she believed it?"

"Repeated brainwashing can do that to a person. To this day, I believe the only thing that saved her was that her husband left. One day. Out of the blue. Told her he was headed out to sea, but never reported for duty, and she never saw him again. Someone said they thought they saw him with a blonde a few days before, but no one knows for sure."

She snorted. "Just like that?"

Cora snapped her fingers. "Just like that."

"Maybe the Karma bus ran him over." Which would be nature's perfect justice.

"Probably. We might get away with stuff for a while, but she eventually comes around."

The door opened behind them, and Bertie stepped out carrying a brown paper bag. "Hazel? Your order is ready."

Hazel stood and took her and Peter's lunch. "Thanks, Bertie."

Cora joined her by the front of the door. "Enjoy your meal, and good luck. You'll have to let me know how it goes."

"I will. Thanks for the luck. I think I might need it."

CHAPTER TWELVE

When Hazel stepped into Peter's office, the bags emitting delicious scents of burgers and fries, she experienced his resulting smile. She knew she'd paved the way to their sticky conversation well. He might want to be angry or annoyed with what she'd tell him, but he couldn't be too mean.

"Hi there." She gifted him with a bright smile as she entered his office. "You should round us up some colas and let the office picnic commence."

He nodded appreciatively. "That sounds like an excellent idea."

He stood, gave her a kiss on the cheek on his way out the door and returned in less than a minute. "This is a nice surprise. Any special reason?"

She hated that he could read her so well. She lifted burgers from the bag and set one in front of each of them. "I missed you and wanted to see you."

"Uh-huh." He unscrewed the cap on his soda, and it hissed in response. "You missed me."

She sent him a wounded look. "Of course, I missed you. And I brought you food, so you should be happy."

"I am happy, but you're rarely this spontaneous unless something has happened."

He shouldn't know her this well. "Fine. A couple of things did happen."

She contemplated starting with Victor's arrival and then using her conversation with Rosalinda as a distraction. But maybe the opposite would work out better.

She hated that she had to talk about Victor at all, but Peter would find out.

She grimaced. "Do you want the bad news first or the only-related-to bad news, but not actually bad first?"

He snorted and shook his head. "You're not making sense."

Here goes nothing. "My ever-loving mother was worried about me, so she sent my ex-boyfriend to town to check on me."

She held her breath and waited.

Peter regarded her for several moments before he spoke. His silence ratcheted up her anxiety. Maybe she shouldn't have said anything after all.

"Well?" she finally prompted.

"I guess my answer depends on how you feel about it. Are you happy to see him? Do you still have feelings?"

She scoffed. "No and not in the least."

He shrugged. "Then what difference does it make?" He bit into his burger.

She squeezed her eyes tightly before she sighed and opened them. "He's not in any hurry to leave. He's already flirting with Cora, and I'm afraid he'll try to cause trouble between us."

Peter swallowed. "I'd say that's up to us. If we don't let him, if we ignore him, what can he really do?"

Hazel didn't want to tell him all the things Victor might do, but maybe she needed to trust Peter and their feelings for each other. "Okay. Well, I just wanted you to be aware."

He studied her for a long moment. "Does he drive a Harley?"

She groaned inside. "Yes."

His expression turned surprised, almost disappointed. "You dated *him*?"

She wouldn't embarrass herself further by admitting she not only dated him, but she'd been madly in love with him. "I was younger then, more naïve."

She'd been angry at her mom for a long time for not protecting her from Victor. Who was she kidding? Her mother was still thrusting Victor in her face. All her mother could see was his power, his potential. Not the jerk beneath.

Hazel understood that she wanted her daughter to marry well, but she'd like a decent person for a husband, too. Her mother would likely not approve of Peter as a match because of his lack of magical abilities. And she really didn't care.

Peter dipped a fry in ketchup. "Don't worry about him. He can't do anything to us. If he misbehaves, he's out of here. Might want to give Cora a heads-up though."

"Already did."

Enough of this line of conversation. "I started making deliveries to Rosalinda at the church this morning."

He laughed and shook his head. "That's convenient. I thought you were avoiding sleuthing from now on."

Her irritation woke, yawned and stretched. "Rosalinda came to *me*. I didn't go anywhere near the church or your investigations until then. Even when I was there, I didn't ask her about anything. I did happen to see a curious list of names on her desk that included Lucy that she promptly hid from me. But she's the one who started talking about Father Christopher first."

He grinned. "I knew you couldn't hold out forever."

She opened her mouth to say something snarky, but he lifted a hand.

"And I've missed you, too. There's nothing like dissecting a case with you."

She shook her head in amazement but smiled. The man could go from annoying to sweet so fast that she couldn't keep up with him.

She opened her soda and drank, giving her brain a chance to catch up with her emotions.

Peter dragged a yellow legal pad closer to him. "Who was on this curious list, and what makes you think it has anything to do with the case?"

In that moment, she realized how much she'd missed discussing cases and bouncing ideas off each other, too. She leaned forward in her chair. "A few things. First was the fact that she hid it from me. Second, she started talking about the case right after she moved the list."

She paused for a sip of soda. "I saw Lucy's name, and Dan Cullpepper."

Peter nodded as he wrote down Lucy and Dan. "Interesting. When we questioned Rosalinda, she said she didn't think anyone from the church had murdered Father Christopher. She mentioned the May Day Curse again, but I don't think traces of peanut end up in a strawberry tart by accident."

"It sounds like most people in town knew of his peanut allergy, unlike me."

He nodded and swallowed. "I'd never heard it before, but I didn't know the Father well. But Rosalinda said his severe peanut allergy was well-known. When I questioned Lucy about it, she said she was aware of it, but that she hadn't used any in her recipe."

Hmm... "Did you check any of her other tarts to see what was in them?"

He pointed a fry at her. "This is why I love you."

Her heart jolted as he shoved the French fry into his mouth. Had he meant the love kind of love, or just the I-love-that-we're-compatible kind of love?

"And?" she prompted.

"Yes, we checked. She had leftover tarts that were made in the same batch, and we tested them. No traces. In fact, we found no traces of peanuts in her kitchen at all."

She worked to clear her mind of his most recent amorous declaration. "Does that mean you're leaning toward someone else having used her strawberry tart as a means to kill him?"

"It's not out of the realm of possibilities."

She really hoped that was true and that Lucy was innocent. "Who would have had access?"

"Anyone who could get into the church's kitchen, so basically anyone that day. Lobster Lucy brought her tarts earlier that morning and put them in the fridge. Then right before the festivities began, she whipped the cream and topped them all."

Hazel put a hand around her throat. "I tried one of them, too. They were delicious. Hard to believe something so sweet could be deadly."

"Deadly to only a select few with that type of allergy. Most anyone else could eat it and be just fine."

Hazel bit into her burger, enjoying the extra pickles Bertie had added for her. She and Peter ate in silence for a few minutes. She stared into his eyes as she pondered the case, mulling over what she knew.

That was until his gaze penetrated her mind and moved into her soul. Then she blinked and looked away, not needing the distraction of her body reacting to his presence.

She removed the soda lid and drank. "Is Dan Cullpepper a suspect? Was I right about Rosalinda's list?"

He flipped back to the previous page on the yellow notepad. "Apparently, Dan's daughter had sought counseling from Father Christopher a couple of years ago when she was pregnant by her teenage boyfriend. I don't know what the Father said to her, but she was very upset when she left. The following Sunday, he gave a passionate sermon about the benefits of remaining chaste and the damning consequences if one did not."

More evidence of Father Christopher's cruelty.

"Late that Sunday afternoon, the poor girl committed suicide. This happened not long after my wife died, so the details are a little fuzzy, but I do remember her funeral and being unable to speak with the devastated family. A little too close to home, you know?"

Hazel's heart bled for that poor family and for Peter. "That is so terrible. What kind of person would do that to a child?"

He picked up a pen and tapped it on the pad. "My question exactly. The more I dig, the more I'm discovering his propensity for brutality."

"Rosalinda didn't like him. That's for sure." Hazel pondered for a moment and then met Peter's gaze. "You don't think she could have killed him, do you? I mean she hated the priest she worked for, and then he fired her."

"Can't rule anyone out at this point, but no, I don't think that sweet, little lady murdered Father Christopher."

A relieved grin spread across her face. "And you've ruled me out."

He blew out a breath. "Thank God for that."

"Or the Blessed Mother," she added.

He snorted. "Or the Blessed Mother. Cora says that, too, you know?"

She pasted on an innocent smile. "Really? That's interesting."

"I've actually heard several people in Stonebridge use it occasionally. Right after I moved back here with Sarah, the town went through a phase where some folks actually embraced the town's sordid past and became very interested in the original four witches. Ladies would make elaborate witch hats in a crafting class and parade around town on Saturdays saying things like Blessed

Mother and pretending to cast spells to invoke weather changes. Even my wife made a hat."

Hazel widened her eyes as she listened. "That sounds dangerous."

"It sure would be today. If I remember correctly, Father Christopher came down hard on his followers, telling them they were taunting the devil and inviting evil into their lives. The witchy fun and games died pretty quickly after that."

Hazel had left her own traditional hat at her mother's house. "What happened to Sarah's hat?"

He shrugged and crumpled the empty wrapper from his hamburger. "I'm sure it's with her other things in my attic."

That concerned her a little. "You still have all her things?"

"I haven't wanted to clean out her stuff, up until recently. Hard memories, you know?"

She could only imagine. "I guess it all takes time. When you're ready, you'll do it."

He nodded thoughtfully. "I think I'm ready."

And, once again, they'd entered uncomfortable territory for her. It wasn't that she wanted Peter to pretend that Sarah and the tragedy that resulted in her death hadn't existed. It was just that she didn't quite know what to say when it all came up.

"Does that mean Lucy is still at the top of your list?" she asked.

"For now. But we're looking at others."

That left her feeling a little better. "I also saw the mayor's name on Rosalinda's list of suspects, if that's what that was."

He tilted his head from side to side as though pondering. "She didn't mention his name to me, but maybe she had her reasons. Also, investigating my boss without endangering my job could be tricky."

Understandable. "Maybe one of your guys could poke around. Then you'd be the buffer to protect him in case the mayor fires back."

He leaned back in his chair and chuckled. "Perfect. I know exactly who to choose. John Bartles wants to redeem himself, so let's see how he does with this assignment. I won't hang him out to dry, but if he hangs himself, that might be better for all involved."

Hazel hated to mess with Karma like that, but if John followed protocol and used common sense, he'd be fine.

Although, she wasn't certain he could.

CHAPTER THIRTEEN

Hazel sat with one leg curled under her, Clarabelle's spell book in one hand, and Glenys' tome open on her lap. "Eye of newt," she mumbled and then lifted her gaze to where Mr. Kitty sat on the edge of the armchair reading with her.

"Who the heck uses eye of newt, and where would I ever find it?"

Mr. Kitty gave her a sassy blink and then looked back at the book in her lap.

She shook her head, frustrated and annoyed. Learning to cast spells using instructions and ingredients three hundred years old was impossible.

Not impossible.

She huffed at her cat, and he huffed back.

Annoyed, she flipped back a few pages in Clarabelle's book, looking for the section on protective spells. After the disaster with Glenys, that was one area she knew she needed to improve upon if she intended to stay in Stonebridge.

Although only some of the protective spells involved blood magic, they still made her a lot more nervous than the earlier ones. She turned back even more pages. Maybe she should try to make it rain. That could always come in handy during a drought, or maybe she could use it to deluge an enemy so that she could get away.

Though she'd have to learn to focus it on one person for that to be effective.

Loud pounding on her front door startled her and sent Mr. Kitty running for cover beneath the couch. She quickly closed both books, glanced about the room for a good hiding place, and decided to set them on the floor and cover them with a quilt.

She hurried to her front door and peeked out the hole, surprised to find Peter on the other side.

He pounded again before she could open it. When she did unlock it and twisted the knob, he pushed through, forcing her backward.

He slammed the door hard behind him seconds before something squishy hit it. His breaths came faster than usual, and water dripped from his hair and shirt.

She gasped. "What on earth?"

"I'm being attacked." He pushed her aside and peered out the peephole. He flinched, and something else hit her door.

She stepped to the window and caught sight of several teenage boys who'd taken cover behind the neighbor's shrubs. "By kids?"

She chuckled, and Peter shot her an irritated look. "With water balloons. I'm the police chief. How dare they?"

"Apparently, they dare."

Peter pushed the mike on the radio on his shoulder. "I need a unit to patrol around Hazel's house. We have some hoodlums ransacking the neighborhood."

Hazel controlled her laughter while he finished his call. Then she cracked up again. "Hoodlums ransacking the neighborhood?"

He looked affronted. "I could get them for assaulting a police officer."

She tucked in her lips and nodded. "They should be very afraid."

He turned to her with a fuming look. "How would you like to get ambushed by a bunch of kids while walking up to my doorstep?"

She should probably quit teasing him, but it was so darned irresistible. "It's only holy water. Maybe they needed to be sure you weren't a witch."

"Yeah, well, this whole holy water thing needs to stop. People are getting out of control."

She peeked out the window again, looking for signs of them. "They're only kids."

At the sound of a motorcycle engine racing away, she jerked her gaze to the opposite end of the street and caught side of a shiny black Harley with a hotter than sin dude driving away.

That didn't mean Victor had been involved in Peter's attack, but she'd bet her best broom that he wasn't innocent.

She turned back to Peter and snickered again. "Looks like they're gone, and you're safe now."

A smile hovered in the corner of his mouth. "You think this is funny?"

She tried to hold back a chuckle but failed. "Kind of."

He lifted his chin in acknowledgement and stepped toward her. "We'll see about that."

She tried to fake to the left and head to the right, but he caught her around the waist anyway. She laughed and pushed against his soaked shirt in protest. "You're getting me all wet."

Laughter danced in his eyes as he stared hard into hers. Her heartbeat raced to catch up with his and then fell into undeniable synchronization.

"It's only a little water," he whispered and lowered his mouth to hers.

Heat and desire whipped through her, and she fought to keep her senses straight. When need threatened to overwhelm her, she pushed against his chest.

A breathless laugh slipped from her, and she ran a hand down her damp shirt. "That was some kiss, officer."

He grinned. "Liked that, did you?"

She should have never let him know how much he affected her. "Just a little."

He chuckled then. "Do you have a towel I can use?"

Hazel pulled a towel from the linen closet and returned to him. "I hope you caught a glimpse of their faces."

"Not one," he said with disappointment. "I was halfway to your doorstep when they started launching a million a minute. I didn't want one in the face, so I ducked and ran."

"Good thing they didn't catch you in a dark alley." She turned her lips into a teasing smile.

"Uh-huh." He scrubbed the towel over his short hair, making it stand straight up. She ran her fingers over it, smoothing the strands.

"I stopped by to see if you wanted to go for ice cream, but I think it might be safer to stay indoors for now."

She schooled her features into a serious look and nodded. "Probably for the best. If you want, I could toss your shirt in the dryer."

Which would leave him shirtless again, but she wouldn't complain.

"It's not that wet."

"It's wet enough to be uncomfortable if you plan on hanging out."

He sighed. "Fine." His fingers went to work on the buttons.

When he'd removed his shirt and undershirt and handed them to her, she paused a moment to give him an obvious stare of appreciation. Her grin turned saucy, and then she headed to her dryer.

"Be careful when you look at a man like that," he called after her.

She changed from her damp shirt into a soft cotton tank while she was at it and returned with her silky pink robe in hand. "You can wear this if you'd like."

He snorted. "First of all, I don't wear pink. Second, I doubt my arms will fit."

She glanced over him again, appreciating his amazing biceps this time, and then tossed the robe aside. "You're probably right."

He turned and reached for the quilt on the floor.

"Wait," she said, but it was already too late. He'd lifted the quilt, revealing the two ancient tomes on the floor.

He glanced to her with a questioning gaze and then back to them. "What's this?"

She hurried forward and picked them up, holding them close to her chest. "Books. Very old books."

He stared at them. "They look like it."

Son of a biscuit. She'd revealed her witchy heritage to him already, but she'd tried to downplay most references to it in her life. At some point, though, she'd have to trust him instead.

She slowly lowered them from her chest. "One is Clarabelle's spell book, and the other belonged to Glenys' relative."

His eyebrows shot up his forehead, and he met her gaze. "How did you end up with hers?"

She crinkled her nose, not wanting to tell him. "Oh, boy. Umm...it's a long story that might involve breaking and entering, although technically the door was unlocked when I went in... Is it illegal to enter if the door isn't locked?"

His gaze grew concerned. "Were you invited in? Did Glenys know you were in her house?"

She shook her head.

"Then yes, it's illegal."

She cast her gaze downward in mock submission. "I can't believe I just confessed that to the police chief."

"Did another witch go with you? Coerce you into entering?"

She glanced up at him. "Does my cat count?"

He dulled his expression. "You're not serious."

"Actually, I am. He talks to me, too."

Peter held up his hands. "Okay, whoa. You're pulling my leg."

She stared at him with a hopeful gaze, and he shook his head in denial.

She hoped she hadn't gone too far. "I probably shouldn't have told you all that so soon. You're not going to run away, are you?"

He hesitated long enough to make her squirm, and then eyed the books in her arms. "I'll stay as long as you let me have a peek inside those."

She snorted. "Your curiosity is as bad as mine."

CHAPTER FOURTEEN

Hazel led Peter to the couch where they sat together. Showing him this intimate part of her life was a huge thing to her, and she hoped he understood that.

She handed Clarabelle's book to him, ignoring the sizzle where her arm bumped his bare skin. "This one belongs to my family. To Clarabelle."

He gently took it from her but didn't open it. "Passed down through generations?"

She shook her head. "Mr. Kitty showed me where it had been hidden in Clarabelle's house, quite possibly since she'd lived there."

He lifted a doubtful brow, and she shrugged. "I'm telling the truth. I was quite shocked to find it, too. It happened that day when I'd twisted my ankle. Mr. Kitty had knocked me down the stairs and that's where I found it. Hidden beneath one of the steps. I can show you the space sometime."

"Fascinating," he said under his breath. He glanced at her. "May I?"

She nodded.

He lifted the cover, trailed a finger down the page. "Better to follow your heart, or you're already dead."

She leaned closer to him and scanned the writing. "I guess that's the motto she lived by."

"Sounds like some wise words."

His skin was warm, his arm strong, and she soaked up the heat. "There are other words in there that might not be so wise...or at least not nice. Scary things."

He angled a sideways glance at her. "What do you mean?"

She held his gaze, waiting for his reaction. "Blood spells. Dark magic."

"Stuff that really works?"

She twisted a strand of hair around her finger. "Possibly. There are spells or parts of spells that coincide with the draining of Redemption Pond where the town tried to drown them. The Witches' Wrath. Others."

The air tightened, and she drew a section of her hair across her lips. She feared at any moment, he'd say he'd heard enough and run for the hills.

"You're telling me the crazy lore that everyone goes on about is real?"

She swallowed. "I don't exactly know since I wasn't there, but it seems like maybe. Some of Clarabelle's spells are only partial spells and ingredients. The rest seem to be in the other book."

"Have you tried them?"

She scoffed and leaned back. "No, I haven't tried them. Are you crazy? I tried that truth-telling spell on myself before I used it on Glenys to get her to confess, and I nearly spilled my entire guts to Charlie Rossler. I might as well have given him complete access to my diary."

One side of Peter's mouth lifted. "I'd like to read your diary."

She elbowed him but smiled. "I don't know why. There's nothing in there about you."

He gave her a wounded look. "Nothing?"

"Okay, maybe a little."

He grinned. "I bet there's a lot more than that."

"We are not talking about my diary. Not when we have three-hundred-year-old tomes right in front of us."

"I'm more interested in your diary," he teased.

She cleared her throat. "Pay attention. I'm trying to tell you about another that turned my irises purple."

He narrowed his gaze. "I remember that. You said it was because you wore contacts."

She lifted her hands in defeat. "What else was I going to say? That I'd practiced witchcraft and screwed up a spell?"

He chuckled. "Yeah...probably not."

"The only other thing I've done besides those and what you witnessed with Glenys was a money spell. That only earned me five bucks."

"Sounds like you need to get better at this. We could retire early."

She liked the way his words hinted that they might grow old together. "Trust me. To get any great benefit from that one, you'd have to pay a hefty cost. Besides, it's blood magic. Always dangerous."

He scowled. "You tried blood magic? I thought that was bad."

Shame nipped at her. She'd always promised her mother she'd steer clear. "Only a small spell, and only because Mr. Kitty wouldn't stop nagging me to learn."

Peter glanced about the room. "Where is he? Do you think he'd talk to me?"

"I'm pretty sure you don't want him to. He never has anything good to say. Although," she added grudgingly. "He did save my butt a few times. Another witch in town says he's Clarabelle's cat who's never died."

He shook his head and gave a sarcastic laugh. "That might be a little too much to believe."

She agreed with a nod. "I have to wonder if he's an offspring, too. But he does have some amazing abilities."

She paused for a moment and then reached up to touch his cheek. "Thank you for letting me share this with you. It's been so hard to keep it all inside."

"I thought you had other witchy friends."

"One friend, remember? And I haven't dared tell her everything. Not about the tomes, especially. I do trust her, but this town can make people crazy." She waved a finger over the spell books. "I'm not sure about any of this, and I don't want to share until I am."

His expression softened. "But you'll share it with me?"

She stared into his eyes, practically feeling the threads between them growing, and she nodded. "I've wanted to before now, but I didn't know what you'd think."

"It's all pretty incredible. That's for sure. But I believe you, Hazel. And I believe in you."

Her heart melted like chocolate over a flame. She leaned closer, and he claimed her lips in the sweetest kiss she'd ever experienced. This falling in love stuff was so much more than she'd expected, but so amazing, too.

He released her and glanced at the books. "Can we try a spell?"

A jolt of panic knocked her. "Here? Now?"

"Why not?"

"Because what if something goes wrong? I know tons about potions and healthy spells. The rest of this is all new, and messing with it scares me. I could blow up the house."

He chuckled. "Not if you do a little one. On me. I'll volunteer."

"You, Chief Parrish, are insane."

He slid an arm around her shoulders and pulled her to him. The back of her arm slid against his strong chest, sending more shivers cascading through her. "You, Miss Hardy, should never underestimate yourself. You said your cat's pushing you to know more. You're not going to learn your strength if you don't practice. It's how everything in life works. Don't be scared. Just respect your heritage, but don't trust it blindly. I know you have good instincts. Follow them."

She shook her head. "I can't do anything to you. What if I turn you into a frog?"

"Then you can kiss me to turn me back."

She gave him a dull stare. "Not funny."

"Fine." He glanced about the room. "What about my shirt? I'm sure it's still wet. Is there something in the books that can make it dry?"

She might have seen a spell in the early, less volatile section. "Maybe."

He jumped up, catching her off guard, and she almost toppled. "I'll get my shirt, and you find it."

He was off, and she stared at the books with trepidation pulsing through her veins. He was right in that she needed to practice more. She would never dare try to master a stronger spell until she'd done well with easier ones. But still...

The moment he stepped into the room, she turned the page and found what she was looking for.

"Got one?"

She stared at him for a long, indecisive moment, and then begrudgingly answered. "Yes."

"Great." He held the shirt out to her. "Are we going to do it right here? Do you need anything for it?"

"A blue and a red candle. One to represent water and the other fire. Then I just need to repeat the words in the right order."

His features fell. "I don't suppose you have those colors of candles, do you?"

Something about his boyish curiosity charmed her. "I'm a witch, aren't I?" she said with a fair amount of sass. "I might not have eye of newt, but I have candles."

She walked to her bedroom, shocked that she'd allowed him to know so much about her. Now, she'd be showing him the tools of her trade. If she wasn't careful, she'd be letting him cook in her cauldron.

He watched as she lifted the suitcase from the closet and placed it on the bed. A small grin tilted his lips when she unzipped the secret compartment and revealed numerous candles, crystals, and dried sage. "You know, you're like the coolest girlfriend I've ever had."

She gasped a laugh. "Okay. And here I thought you'd arrest me or something if you saw this."

He lifted his brows flirtatiously. "I'm not going to arrest you, but I might 'something'."

She snorted. "Let's be serious here. In a few moments, we might be standing outside calling the fire department."

He took the candles from her. "Don't worry so much. Are we doing this in the kitchen?" Before she could answer, he left her bedroom, as excited as a kid with a new toy.

First, she required a promise from him to be serious and not interrupt her while she practiced. He agreed, placed his shirt on the counter in front of them, and stood back to give her space.

She felt utterly ridiculous as she scanned the rest of the spell. She could do this.

With that thought in mind, she closed her eyes and took a few deep breaths to clear her head. When peace settled over her, she didn't look at Peter as she pulled a long wooden match from the box she kept.

She struck the match against the side of the box, sending the strong scent of sulfur into the air. "Water, a gift from the sea, I ask that you take it back to thee." She held the flame close to the blue wick until it caught fire.

Her nerves crested, and she took a moment to search for peace again.

She swallowed. "Fire, chase away the rain, to where it waits to come back again. I send to the Blessed Mother this plea. Make dry this shirt, so mote it be."

She lit the red candle, and both flames leapt high into the air and danced wildly, causing Peter to grab her arm and pull her back a step.

"Is it done?" he whispered.

Her emotions ran high, and she slipped her fingers between his and held on. "Let the flames die down," she whispered as they bonded closer to each other.

She didn't need Cora to tell her that allowing Peter to watch her perform magic would have consequences. She should have known it would.

Good consequences if they stayed together.

Bad, if they didn't.

The flickering flames finally slowed and returned to normal. She stepped forward, inhaled, and blew them out.

Peter lifted the shirt and squeezed it in several places. "Oh, my God. It's dry."

She smiled, allowing herself the smallest bit of pride. "Blessed Mother, it is."

He grinned and lifted the shirt, sliding his arm into the sleeve. "It's really dry."

She waited for the reality of her curse and how she'd screwed it up to appear, but miraculously, it didn't.

With his smile still in place, he buttoned up the shirt and then turned in a circle for her to see. "I'm sending all my laundry to you from now on. You could have it clean and dry in two seconds."

She teased him with a snort. "Don't get ahead of yourself, buddy. I'm not interested in being anyone's maid."

His features dropped, but she could still sense the playfulness inside. "Dang. What's the point of having a cool girlfriend if she doesn't share her skills?"

Intense happiness radiated from her heart, and she slipped her hands around his neck. "This." She stood on tiptoe and pressed her lips against his.

Several moments later, he broke their kiss and chuckled. "I guess that is pretty sweet."

CHAPTER FIFTEEN

As Hazel pedaled, her gaze flitted from the riot of white and purple wildflowers growing in Mrs. Jackson's yard along the white picket fence to the bird taking flight from a nearby tree. Only a few fluffy clouds played in the crystal blue sky. And once again, she couldn't imagine calling anywhere else home.

She coasted as she neared the corner by the church, enjoying the wind blowing through her curls. She might regret the decision to not secure them with a band, but for now, nothing could mar this perfect day.

Except the sight of kids selling holy water balloons on the street corner and Victor planting geraniums near the main entrance to the church. She blinked, trying to find words, but none would come.

He glanced up as she approached and dismounted her bike. A flat of pink, orange and purple zinnias rested next to him on the grass, along with another flat of red geraniums. He squinted against the bright sun as their gazes connected.

Irritation thumped hard inside her like tennis shoes in a dryer. "What in the Samhain are you doing?"

She was starting to sound like a broken record where he was concerned.

One corner of his mouth quirked. "Good morning, goddess. You look amazing."

She ignored the familiar bleep of long-ago attraction. On the surface, Victor was the perfect package, but she knew what lay beneath. "Answer my question."

He opened his palm, gesturing toward the garden. "Planting flowers, obviously. I would think an earth witch would appreciate that."

She narrowed her gaze in distrust. He couldn't have known she'd be stopping by to drop off tea to Rosalinda this morning, so what was his game? "I can see that. My question is why."

With one lithe move, he stood, and she now had to angle her gaze upward to see him. "I'm new in town. I want to make a good impression. As you know, some residents are on a particularly nasty witch hunt, so I'm trying to avoid suspicion." He nodded toward the kids selling water balloons.

She couldn't very well cast blame since she'd joined the chowder cook-off for the same reason. "It sounds like you've met Timothy."

Easy laughter rolled off his tongue. "Yeah, I've met the dude. Does he not realize his blood is the same as ours?"

Hazel had always been jealous of his ability to know things instantly. "He knows. His family denied their heritage a long time ago, and he's keeping up the tradition. However, very few in town know he is. Certainly, none of the witch haters."

"I could take him out for you if you'd like." He snapped his fingers.

Dang it. She'd love dearly to say yes in that instance, but she didn't want Victor involved. Didn't want him in town at all. "Thanks, but no. We're dealing with it." For now, anyway.

"Yeah. Besides, that's *your* challenge."

His words confused her. "What do you mean?" Her personal challenge or the town's?

"Nothing. Just..." He shrugged. "Not my problem."

Her anxieties twitched, and she forced herself to ignore his taunts and relax. She couldn't let him upset her. That gave him control. "It's an interesting situation here in Stonebridge."

He hooked a thumb into his jeans and regarded her with interest. "Yeah?"

She'd wanted to have this conversation with Peter the night before, but she'd never found the perfect opportunity, and she wasn't sure he could have helped her anyway. "Three hundred years ago, the town persecuted four elemental witches."

"I'm aware of the history."

Of course, he would be. "One of them was my ancestral grandmother. One of the curses those witches placed upon the town, who so desperately wanted to rid society of our kind, was that someone with their blood would always live here. It's a losing battle to try to get rid of us, but they don't know that."

"Interesting." He nodded, his icy blue eyes sparking as he thought. "I like this grandmother of yours. Wish I could have met her."

No way would she tell him he still could meet her ghost.

"So," she continued. "There should be four of us here now, right? Belinda recently passed. Well, was murdered. Another, Glenys the bank manager, was sent away for murdering the first one. There's me, of course, and the final person is our favorite, Timothy the librarian."

He chuckled. "Oh, wow. That is rich. Is he aware of this curse?"

"Of course not. I'm not going to out myself to a witch hater by telling him."

"He's a witchy witch hater," he corrected.

"Whatever. What really has me concerned is who will replace the dead one, and if the other is still alive but not in Stonebridge, will someone come along for her, too? How can I find out?"

His gaze turned sultry, putting her on alert. "Want me to look into it for you?"

Inwardly, she groaned. What had she been thinking?

No, she didn't want him involved, and she never should have mentioned it to him. Heck, never should have spoken to him at all. If she wanted him to leave, she needed to make it the most boring place on Earth.

She did her best to give him a carefree smile. "No. I'm just musing. Didn't mean to take up your time."

With her common sense back in place, she retrieved the tin of tea from her basket and headed toward the church's door.

Suddenly, a doomed feeling claimed her. What if Victor was the replacement? Please, Blessed Mother. No.

"Try researching online."

His suggestion stopped her, and she turned back. "Like one of those ancestry websites?" Why hadn't she thought of that?

He knelt and picked up the hand shovel. "Why not? It's not reserved for non-witches. Research the people already in town, and then check any new ones who arrive. That should give you plenty of heads-up notice, so you can be ahead of the game."

She growled inside, hating that he could read her so well. "Thanks. I think I'll do that."

She lifted a hand and let it drop. "Later."

"For sure," he called after her. Unfortunately, she was afraid that would be true.

Cooler air scented by time and overwhelming quiet greeted her as she entered the church. She glanced at the gorgeous, empty chapel as she passed, and chanced opening her senses again to the multitude of souls that had worshipped here. For the most part, happiness reigned, but darker emotions clung to the shadows.

She knocked on Rosalinda's mostly-closed office door and peeked inside. The room was empty. Granted, Rosalinda wouldn't be expecting her until later, but Hazel had decided to make the church her first stop instead of the last today.

Mostly because she was eager to talk to the church's secretary again and see if she could extract more information. Now, she'd have to come back later with her delivery or leave the tea and wait until next week to speak to Rosalinda.

Her curiosity wouldn't allow her to wait.

She checked down hallways and in other rooms to be sure Rosalinda wasn't somewhere else in the church, but the whole building seemed to be empty.

With the tea canister in hand, she headed back outside, wishing she didn't have to see Victor again. Calm and boring, she reminded herself as she pushed open the door.

Victor glanced up, and the enchanting smile returned to his face. "That was fast."

"Rosalinda isn't here."

"I could have told you that."

She wanted to be irritated that he hadn't, but he couldn't have known.

"She left about ten minutes ago. Had to drive some papers to the regional office in Salem."

The gears in her brain turned. "To Salem? She'll likely be gone for at least a half hour." And that was if Rosalinda didn't stay to chat, which was unlikely.

"No idea." He pointed toward the flat of flowers farthest from him. "Could you hand me a couple of geraniums?"

She snorted. "Since when do you know the names of plants?"

"Since I fell in love with an earth witch a couple of years ago."

Oh, no. She was not getting drawn into this again. He'd had his chance and had completely blown it.

Besides, she loved Peter, and what she had with him was much deeper and richer than the superficial love affair she'd had with

Victor. She thought she'd been in love with him. Now, she realized she'd been in love with the idea of him.

Something her mother apparently still clung to.

She nudged the flat of flowers closer to him, ignoring his claim of affection. "Could you do me a favor?"

"Absolutely. See, I knew you'd need me."

She worked to keep a delirious laugh to a minimum. "I need to check something inside the church, but I don't want anyone to see me doing it. If someone shows up, will you escort them inside and make a lot of noise, so I hear you coming?"

Intrigue flashed across his face. "Ooh. I like this daring side of you. Maybe later we can take a ride on my Harley, and you can tell me what you're up to."

She held up a hand and chuckled. The man was relentless. "Please. I just need you to keep a look out. Can you do that?"

He winked. "That and so much more."

If he wasn't such a shallow person, she'd be flattered.

"Thanks," she said before she rolled her eyes and walked off.

CHAPTER SIXTEEN

Hazel's pulse throbbed with excitement as she hurried back to Rosalinda's office. The woman had been more than a little secretive last time, and Hazel was dying to know what she might have hidden.

She dropped the tea canister on the corner of the desk and claimed Rosalinda's chair. She tugged on the biggest drawer, looking for files, but it was locked. "Son of a crunchy biscuit." The larger filing cabinet behind her was tightly secured, too.

With nervous fingers, she opened the pencil drawer and searched it for keys. She looked under the potted plant, behind the pencil sharpener, and even lifted pictures from the wall to see if anything would fall out.

Frustration reigned.

Rosalinda must keep them with her.

Here, Hazel had the perfect opportunity and could do nothing with it.

Then another idea slid into her consciousness like a slimy slug, and she sagged against the chair. She had no choice.

With dread weighing each of her footsteps, she headed back outside.

"Victor?" She did her best to sound sweet instead of annoyed. "Could I ask you for one more favor?"

His satisfied grin nearly stole her composure. "Anything, goddess."

She swallowed an unkind retort. "Can you open a locked drawer?"

He stood. "Drawers. Doors. Anything you want."

She motioned him forward. "Hurry, then."

With a few muttered words and some deep concentration, he had both drawers opened within seconds.

"Thank you so much." She plopped into Rosalinda's seat again and tugged open the drawer. She discovered a jar of peanut butter, a can of almonds, and a big bag of Swiss chocolate. Some might consider it a payday, but she didn't have food on her mind today. "Nothing but snacks."

He slid open a drawer on the larger filing cabinet. "Try here. You might have more luck."

With renewed determination, she moved next to him and glanced over the folder's tabs. Immediately, she recognized the names of many in town that had been moved to the front of the files. Lobster Lucy Flanigan—she couldn't believe they'd included lobster as part of her name. Dan Cullpepper and Family. The mayor and his wife, Robert and Sandra Elwood. "Thank you. This is perfect."

She turned to him with a bright grin and then dimmed it when she saw his reaction. "You're a great friend. Thanks so much."

He snorted. "You're trying to friend-zone me now?"

She wanted to explode, to tell him once again what a jerk he'd been, that he'd be lucky if she did call him friend, but she was done traveling that road. "I have a boyfriend, Victor. In case you've forgotten."

"Yeah. One who has absolutely zero powers. Not much of anything, really. He'll never keep you happy."

She narrowed her gaze, anger flitting through the cracks. "Did you check up on him?"

"Did you think I wouldn't?"

Full-blown ire took over. "You have no right to interfere in my life. You lost that privilege when I found you with Adele, naked in my bed in case you've forgotten. I don't want to hear your opinion whatsoever on my new life and who I choose to share it with. Got it?"

Instead of joining her anger, he grinned. "Do you realize your intensity when you're angry? You should try a spell when something has you pissed. You'd be amazing."

Yeah, like a blood spell directed straight at him. Instead of arguing further, she pointed toward the door. "We're done with this discussion. Go keep watch."

He lifted his chin in agreement. "For now."

The urge to pick up Rosalinda's potted fern and hurl it at his retreating back was strong, but she resisted. Instead, she buried her face in her hands, slid her fingers down her cheeks, and then shook them out as though the action could cleanse Victor's slime from her soul.

Several precious moments slipped past while she regained her sanity and then she snatched the mayor's file. But something gave her pause, and she peered back into the drawer. At the very front, sat a new, pristine-looking folder just asking to be noticed.

She pulled it out, turned, and placed it on Rosalinda's desk. As she glanced through the contents, a big smile erupted on her face. Dealing with Victor's antics had been worth it.

Rosalinda apparently enjoyed sleuthing herself. She had listed each person that had been named as a possible suspect in the case. Some had been crossed out like Hazel's name had, but she'd underlined Lucy, Dan and Mayor Elwood in red. Even the poor woman who'd died in the crash, Karen Bernard, was on the list, on a separate side, albeit. But that made no sense. She was dead.

Hazel flipped the page and found a more detailed list of what Rosalinda knew about Lucy. The next was all about the mayor. She should take notes, so she wouldn't forget anything. With her mind racing, she searched for a blank piece of paper and then realized she could just take a picture and be out of there in a jiffy.

She quickly snapped photos of all the pages. After that, she pulled personal files from the drawer and glanced through them, but it seemed Rosalinda had already condensed anything of interest into the other file. Her lucky day, it seemed.

Hazel replaced the folders in the drawer and closed it. She didn't want to ask Victor to lock them, but she would just so Rosalinda wouldn't suspect anything.

She straightened everything on the desk, hoping it looked the same as when she'd entered. She tucked the canister of tea under her arm, intending to come back later so that if anything was amiss, Rosalinda wouldn't immediately suspect her.

She hurried outside and halted mid-step when she found Rosalinda speaking to Victor. Her heart flopped flat on the sidewalk.

Rosalinda looked up in wonder. "Hazel. I wasn't expecting you until later. What a nice surprise."

She summoned her friendliest smile. "Hello, Rosalinda. I stopped by with your tea, but when you weren't here, I decided to come back with it later so that we could chat, too."

"Oh, darn. I wish I could chat now, but I was on my way to the church in Salem and realized I'd forgotten what I was supposed to deliver. So, I really don't have time now. I need to grab and run."

Hazel waved away her concern. "That's okay. I'll just give you your tea and catch up with you later."

Rosalinda pointed toward the building. "But I need to pay you."

She shook her head. "No worries. I'll stop by later or catch you next time."

Rosalinda's gaze turned odd. "Are you sure?"

"Absolutely. I still have more deliveries to make, so I should be going, too. Safe travels."

Victor sent Hazel a conspiratorial wink and put a hand on Rosalinda's back. "I'll walk in with you. I could use a drink from the water fountain."

She hopped on her bike and pedaled away before Victor or Rosalinda could find a reason to stop her.

When she was half a mile down the road, she pulled to the side and stopped in the shade of a large oak. Her breaths came hard but slowly morphed into crazed chuckles.

Blessed Mother, she couldn't believe how close she'd come to getting caught. She prayed she'd understood Victor's wink to mean he had her back and would lock the drawers. She had no idea what Rosalinda would have done if she'd discovered her, but damage to her reputation would be at the top of her list.

As soon as she was back at the teashop and had sent Gretta to lunch, she'd pull out her phone and study the information she'd gleaned.

Then she'd have to figure out a way to tell Peter what she'd discovered without letting him know she'd broken the law. Again.

CHAPTER SEVENTEEN

In the quiet backroom of the teashop, Hazel studied the photos she'd taken of Rosalinda's abbreviated version of the files. Dan's information was pretty much what she already knew. Lucy's husband had abused her, and Father Christopher had encouraged her to stay in the marriage.

Hazel heaved a disgusted sigh.

Mayor Ellwood and his wife were more interesting. They, too, had undergone counseling with Father Christopher. But, for some unknown reason, he had suggested Sandra leave her husband, that staying with him would damage her soul.

Hazel shook her head as she tried to make sense of the two cases. The more she learned about Father Christopher, the more she wondered if she'd encountered a psychopath who'd hidden behind a priest's clothing.

She continued reading, and then paused when she found Rosalinda had written "unofficial notes" toward the bottom of the page. It appeared that Rosalinda was certain Father Christopher and Sandra Elwood had engaged in an affair years ago.

Beneath that, Rosalinda had noted that the mayor intended to run for state senator, and then she'd added, "possibly killed F.C. to keep him quiet" with a question mark afterward.

Hazel didn't know the mayor well, but Peter did and would have more insight as to whether he believed Mayor Ellwood was capable of murdering the Father to keep him quiet and further his political career. Or maybe it was Sandra who saw the Father as a stumbling block on the way to the Capitol and wanted him gone before someone spotlighted her sordid past.

Interesting. All very interesting.

She hoped Peter would be more interested than angry.

When she'd exhausted that line of information, she moved on to something more personal.

She tapped from the phone's gallery of photos to the browser and typed in a search for ancestry websites. When she found one that appealed to her, she created an account and logged in.

Immediately, she found connections between herself and her mother. Her aunts came up quickly, and she located an entry including a photo of the man who'd fathered her and then had left many, many years ago.

She wrinkled her nose, not liking to think about that part of her history. Or non-history as she liked to call it. He'd never been part of her life, and she had no interest in his or where he might be in the world.

She made it back as far in her research as her great, great grandmother before Gretta returned from lunch, and Hazel hurried to click off the phone screen. Her assistant entered the backroom and stowed her purse in a cubby beneath the counter. "What are you doing?"

Hazel greeted her with a relaxed smile. "Just a little online shopping. How was your lunch?"

"Wonderful. I walked to the park and ate my sandwich while watching the ducks. A few came close, wanting nibbles of bread, but most were busy defending their space on the water."

"Sounds awesome. I should take my lunch in the park, too. Good for the soul."

Hazel studied her assistant, still not happy that she'd felt she needed to test Hazel. But she had to get over that. "Hey, I have some work I need to do back here, so you're going to be on your own up front, okay?"

Gretta gave her a swift nod. "Sure thing, boss." She stacked a few tins of Pineberry Bush tea in her hands and headed out front. Hazel was happy to see that the citizens and tourists all loved her new iced teas.

Instead of getting to work, Hazel pulled up the ancestry website again. This time, though, she searched for Father Christopher's name. She sat back in surprise when she found not only him, but a daughter's name listed. *Karen Bernard.*

She didn't know for a fact that this Karen and the one who'd died in Stonebridge on May Day were the same person. But those odds were too great to ignore.

The bigger question was what were the odds that a woman by that same name had taken up residence in Stonebridge and had died the same day as her father?

Had Karen known Father Christopher was her father? Had she been the one to kill him and then end her own life after she'd set events in motion, and there really was no May Day Curse?

Hazel would be very interested to find out. Peter would be, as well.

When she exhausted every interesting avenue on Father Christopher's side, she returned to the main screen. This time, she typed in Peter's name and began a search on him. She found his parents, grandparents, and Sarah.

Curious, she clicked on Sarah's name and traced her back to her great-great-grandparents. It seemed her family had lived in Pennsylvania for generations. She scrolled over to close out the screen but stopped when the cursor crossed a name that seemed familiar. Ernest Hardy.

She shook her head thinking it weird that she'd encountered that same name on the search of her family, too. It might be a coincidence. Surely, there was more than one Ernest Hardy that had lived in the U.S.

Ignoring the sick feeling building in the pit of her stomach, she found a pen and jotted down his birthdate and parents' names. Then she backed out of Sarah's search and entered her own.

It took her several clicks to find the line that also included Ernest Hardy, and then she stared at the blatant facts staring her straight in the face.

She and Sarah shared ancestry.

Still, that didn't mean that line would trace all the way back to Clarabelle.

But if it did...

She inhaled sharply and clutched her stomach.

Blessed Mother, if it did, that meant Sarah had had to die so that Hazel could find her way to Stonebridge. If she hadn't, Hazel might never have known this world existed.

Might never have fallen for Sarah's husband.

CHAPTER EIGHTEEN

Hazel sat on the couch that evening with her laptop resting on her legs. A notebook with several lines drawn including names and birthdates lay next to her. Mr. Kitty loafed on the back of the couch, peering over her shoulder as though he, too, could read her computer screen.

She'd finished the workday in a fog, skipped dinner, and went straight for the computer instead. She'd been at it several hours, searching different veins of her heritage and writing them all down. Her stomach ached, and her head hurt worse than that. This couldn't be true, couldn't be happening.

The Blessed Mother couldn't be that cruel.

Her phone rang, and she startled. Her actions made Mr. Kitty jump, and he growled in response.

She glanced at the phone screen.

Peter. Poor Peter.

She cleared her throat of emotion. "Hey there."

Hopefully he wouldn't see through the fake veneer that coated her words.

"Hazel. I know it's late, but would it be all right if I stop by. I have something that I want to give to you."

"To me?" She couldn't imagine what it might be. "Sure. I'm still up, so stop by."

He chuckled. "Actually, I'm just pulling up in front of your house now."

She panicked and slammed her laptop shut. "Great. See you in a second."

She hung up and dropped her cell phone. This time, she wouldn't leave evidence where Peter might stumble upon it. She gripped her laptop and hurried into her bedroom where she slipped it beneath the bed.

Peter was already knocking before she made it back into the living room. She quickened her steps and opened the door. The smile on his face came straight from his soul, leaving him with the most handsome, dearest look. She almost cried.

"Hazel." He leaned forward and kissed her cheek.

She stepped back to let him enter, hoping she could keep it together while he was there. She closed the door and eyed the small brown paper sack he had in his hand. "I have to admit, you've piqued my curiosity."

He drew a finger down her cheek and across her lips, drawing shivers from deep inside. "Not a hard thing to do."

"You're one to talk."

His presence lessened her worries, and she tried to put them out of her mind and focus on him. Despite her gut feeling, she had no proof that Sarah belonged to Clarabelle.

He tilted his head toward the couch. "Let's sit." He took her hand and led her to the couch where he sat next to her.

Something about his demeanor left her edgy. "You're making me nervous."

"Nervous, why?"

She narrowed her gaze and shook her head. "I don't know. The energy you're emitting is strong. More so than normal."

He shrugged. "I am kind of excited. I've been sitting on this for a little while, not sure what to do. But after our conversation the other night, when you shared your magic with me, it became very clear."

He placed the bag on her lap, and she wrapped tentative fingers around it.

His words didn't help to settle her frayed nerves. At least his gift didn't feel like a jeweler's box. A marriage proposal would have made things so much worse.

She opened the end of the bag, wrapped her fingers around what felt like a book, and slid it out. Powerful energy reached out to her, and she realized what she experienced wasn't coming from Peter so much as it was from this object.

She opened the front cover and then lifted her gaze to Peter. "Another spell book?"

He nodded. "This one belonged to a woman named Genevieve. I believe the town found her guilty of witchcraft and drowned her."

Hazel's heart thudded in a crazy beat, and she turned several pages. She had seen mention of a Genevieve in Clarabelle's book. They'd crafted spells together. "Blessed Mother, Peter. I think you're right. Where did you get this?"

He scrubbed his chin as he stared at her for a long moment. "If I tell you, you have to promise to never say a word. You could ruin me."

Now, he really had piqued her curiosity. "I promise."

"I found it in Belinda's house when we searched it after her death. I have no idea why I stuck it in my jacket instead of keeping it as evidence of her involvement in witchcraft. Maybe I didn't want to stir more trouble in town. Or maybe I didn't want the investigation messed up by something that might not have been relevant. I regretted it the moment my officers and I left her house, but I couldn't go back. I hid it in my closet after I got home for the day and haven't touched it since."

She snorted. "I'm glad you took it. Can you imagine if this got into the wrong hands?"

"That's what I figured, too." He slipped a hand beneath hers and twined their fingers. "After you shared your dark secrets with me the other night, I knew giving it to you was the right thing."

His faith in her brought tears to her eyes.

"Oh, great." He shifted in his seat and drew a thumb beneath one of her eyes. "I didn't want to make you cry."

She shook her head and sniffed. "Good tears."

He didn't seem convinced.

She placed a hand on his cheek and tried for a smile. "Thank you. It seems weird to now have three spell books from so long ago. Like what am I supposed to do with them?"

He lifted his brows, uncertain. "That part belongs in your court, Miss Hardy. I'm completely clueless. Maybe you'll find better or easier spells in it."

If Genevieve was anything like Clarabelle and Glenys' grandmother, she was certain that wouldn't be the case.

She fingered the edge of the blue leather tome. A year ago, she never could have pictured herself in this quaint, lovely town with a handsome police chief who seemed to like her very much, and be the owner of not one, but three ancient spell books. One choice in her life had led to so many dramatic changes.

She glanced up to catch his expression. "I've been thinking about the descendants of the other witches. Now that Belinda's gone, someone else must be coming to take her place or is already living here in Stonebridge."

Thoughts of how she'd come to be in town tried to push their way to the surface, but she squashed them.

"Eliza's book belonged to Glenys who is still alive, but whoever takes Belinda's place should maybe have this book. But neither

Glenys or Belinda were very good people, and I wouldn't want to give it to someone who isn't."

"You're worrying a lot about chickens before the egg hatches."

She narrowed her gaze and snorted at the ridiculous phrase.

He nudged her with his shoulder. "I mean it. What if, on the other hand, the next person to come along is great, someone you trust, someone that could partner with you and help you with spells? Someone who could help make Stonebridge a better place?"

She hadn't considered that side of it. She'd absolutely love to have someone she could trust in addition to Cora. "I just don't know how to figure out who it is."

"Maybe you have to wait for that person to tell you."

She nodded thoughtfully. "Maybe so. But what if she's like me and has no clue? What if she's lived here for a long time and never knew?"

What if his dead wife had lived this close to her heritage without knowing?

"I guess that's possible."

Her throat closed so tight it hurt. *What if that was why Sarah had been the victim of a hit and run? What if someone had found out, and they'd murdered her?*

She couldn't continue down this vein of thought right now and maintain control over her emotions. She inhaled several slow breaths, working to release the anxiety that threatened to overwhelm her.

Enough of this discussion. She had other things to confess. "I'm kind of glad that you told me you stole Belinda's book."

"Why's that?"

"Because I have something to tell you, too, and it may or may not include breaking the law."

He shifted and scolded her with a stern look. "You didn't."

She bit her bottom lip, hoping for understanding, and nodded. "I mean I didn't technically break into any buildings. Or even Rosalinda's office for that fact. But I may have broken into her files. Is that still illegal?"

He closed his eyes and shook his head. "I should put you in a jail cell for a night to teach you a lesson so that you don't keep putting yourself into situations like this."

"I'm sorry," she said earnestly. "I couldn't help it. I just knew she'd kept information about Father Christopher from me when I was in her office the other day, and I needed to know what it was."

He lifted a disagreeing brow. "You didn't *need* to know. You wanted to."

She waved away his clarification. "Semantics. Anyway, I found a file that she'd been keeping on all the people who were possible suspects. She'd compiled several notes from their original files and then added her own thoughts and speculations. I think she might be trying to figure out who the killer is, too."

"Oh, great. Now, I have two novices to worry about."

She frowned. "I'm not a novice. I've helped you successfully solve three other cases, remember? In fact, if it wasn't for me, Glenys would still be strutting around town planning the end of life in Stonebridge as we know it."

He wrapped an arm around her shoulder and squeezed her tight against him. "May I remind you that you could have gotten us killed in the process?"

Like she would ever forget that. But that wasn't the point right now. "Again, semantics. I'm a capable person who helps with cases. Rosalinda is a meddling, old woman."

She waved her hands in front of them, mimicking erasing their conversation to that point. "Forget all that. Don't you want to know what I learned?"

He straightened, and she knew she had him. "I took pictures of the pages. Most of it was information we already know about, but I learned something interesting about the mayor's wife."

Hazel paused for a moment for effect. *"She had an affair with Father Christopher."*

His eyes flew open wider. "She what?"

She pointed a finger at him. "Just as I thought. Rosalinda *didn't* tell you that information, either, did she?"

He scowled. "No, she did not."

"I swear, that docile old lady is up to something. You'd better keep an eye on her before she gets into trouble."

He lifted his chin in agreement. "I want to hear more about the mayor's wife."

She filled him in on the sparse details of their affair. "There wasn't that much in there other than Rosalinda speculated that someone else found out about them years later and had blackmailed Father Christopher. She guessed that's why some of the money had gone missing from the church. That was right about the time the Father fired Rosalinda, so I'm wondering if he tried to blame her."

Peter drew a hand down his face. "I need a pen and paper to write this all down."

If he'd been in uniform, he would have had his trusty notepad in his pocket.

"Don't worry. I'll send you a message with all the information and pass along the pictures, too, so you can see everything."

He didn't seem particularly thrilled with her answer. "Okay, but don't forget. I'd like to look at it as soon as possible."

She turned on her phone to forward the photos. When it opened to the website where she'd been searching family trees, she panicked and nearly dropped it trying to close out the screen.

But seeing it reminded her of what else she'd discovered on the website besides her possible connection to Sarah. "Oh, my gosh,

Oh, my gosh. Oh, my gosh. Forget about what I learned at Rosalinda's."

She squeezed his hand to get him to fully focus. "Peter. You are not going to believe this, but Karen Bernard was Father Christopher's daughter."

He stared at her for several endless moments, his expression blank. "You're kidding me."

"Nope." She grinned, trying not to let pride in her sleuthing skills go to her head.

"That's too much of a coincidence."

"Agreed. I've tried, but I can't figure out the connection between the two deaths. Still, it seems like there has to be one."

"Yeah." He leaned his head against hers. "I'll get right on that, too, in the morning."

CHAPTER NINETEEN

Hazel left her house the next morning and followed the familiar path into town. She wouldn't be doing tea deliveries and the weather was perfect, so she opted to walk, which would give her a chance to work through some things that she hadn't managed to sort that morning.

The information she'd learned from Rosalinda had been the front-runner in her mind. Once she'd tamed that train of thought, she'd turned to thinking repeatedly about what Peter had said concerning making friends with a possible new witch.

She'd also taken what he'd said about worrying about chickens and applied it to the research on connecting her and Sarah's heritage. Many times, she'd discovered a connection between herself and an unlikely person, only to comment on how small the world really was.

Sarah could be her relative without Sarah being in Clarabelle's direct line, and then she didn't need to worry about the world caving in on her.

She kept these thoughts in mind as she made her way to the bank that morning. No reason to fret over a disaster that hadn't happened. She needed to live in the moment, and this moment was all about checking on the status of her soon-to-be new house.

Or at least, she hoped Clarabelle's house would be hers soon.

Her happiness dimmed when she recognized the sandy-haired average built officer walking half a block ahead of her on the opposite side of the street, and she slowed her steps.

John Bartles. A man she never cared to see again. Especially not this morning when she didn't feel particularly partial to conjuring her fake, non-witch personality.

When John stopped quickly and slipped between two buildings, her curiosity came alive like a zombie during the apocalypse. That was odd behavior for one of Stonebridge's finest, even if it was John.

She continued walking, trying to see if he was hiding or if he'd taken a side street to the alley behind.

A few seconds later, he peeked around the corner of the building, and then started walking again. She glanced up the sidewalk ahead of John and recognized the mayor and his wife strolling in the same direction.

Was this John trying to carry out orders to investigate the mayor by stalking him and his wife? Not that she was above something similar, but she would have done a much better job at hiding.

When he repeated his movements, this time turning to face a store window as though he was interested in what was behind the glass, she really did begin to wonder about his antics. She chuckled. He'd been cuckoo as of late, but now she wondered if he'd lost his ever-loving mind.

She glanced toward the mayor again and inhaled in gleeful surprise. The mayor was no longer walking away but striding toward Officer Bartles with an angry expression on his face.

Oh, boy. This should be good.

She glanced up and down the street to ensure no cars were coming and stepped off the sidewalk to cross the road. There was no way she'd miss this confrontation.

The mayor reached John seconds before she stepped onto the cobblestone sidewalk fifty feet from where they stood, and she paused.

Mayor Elwood jabbed John hard in the chest. "What in the sam hell do you think you're doing? If you weren't the law, I'd be calling the cops right now."

John's face blanched. "Sorry, sir. I'm only strolling down the street."

"If that's so, then why do you hide every time I glance backward? You've been tailing us for four blocks."

The mayor's wife placed her hand on his forearm. "Come on, Robert. I think you're overreacting." She was a gentle, almost fragile blonde, but she seemed quite capable of handling him.

John seemed relieved, but the mayor shook his head angrily. "I am not overreacting, Sandra. This isn't the first time this imbecile has harassed us, and I've had enough. We're marching down the street and talking to your boss right now."

Hazel cringed. Poor Peter.

Sandra graced her husband with a patient smile. "We have things to get done this morning, Robert, and don't have time for this nonsense."

He puffed out his chest, and then she seemed to shrink back. "Fine. You can handle the bank matters while I deal with this. It won't take long."

Without waiting for her reply, he gripped John's forearm and walked away.

Mrs. Elwood sighed in exhaustion and turned toward the bank. Hazel hurried to catch up to her.

"Good morning, Mrs. Elwood."

Sandra Elwood glanced her way with a kind smile, but Hazel sensed her fatigue and resignation. "Good morning, Hazel. Sorry about the scene. My husband has been under a lot of stress lately."

"I'm sure, with him preparing to run for senator. That must be a lot of work, and what just happened isn't the best publicity. If it helps, there are not many people out, and I don't think anyone else noticed."

She shook her head in dismay. "Let's hope not."

Hazel had always liked the mayor's wife with her quiet charm and concern for the citizens. She had a heck of a time picturing her having an affair with Father Christopher. Even though that had occurred years ago, the woman seemed too smart for that.

They had almost reached the bank, and Hazel panicked when her opportunity was only moments from slipping away. "Would you mind talking with me for a minute?"

Mrs. Elwood glanced toward the bank.

"In private?" Hazel added. "I know you're in a hurry, but I have some sensitive things to say and wouldn't want anyone to overhear."

The woman's defenses shot up like a bullet aimed toward the sky. "Excuse me?"

Hazel offered her a friendly smile and hoped it would smooth the edges. "I've come across some information regarding Father Christopher that involves you, and I'd like to give you a heads-up."

She'd also like to see how she reacted.

Ice chilled Mrs. Elwood's gaze. "Do I need to call my husband back?"

Hazel extended a hand toward the mayor's wife but didn't touch her. "Please. I'm not trying to threaten you. I just want to talk, to tell you what I've heard."

She seemed hesitant but nodded. They stepped away from the bank's door, and Mrs. Elwood faced her with a wary gaze.

Hazel exhaled a tense breath. "Is it true that you once had an affair with Father Christopher?"

All color disappeared from her face. "Where did you hear that?"

"I can't reveal my source, but information was found in church records."

"That—" She clamped her lips shut and shook her head. "Father Christopher told me he would keep our secret."

Hazel sent her a commiserating look. "I'm not sure who or if he told, but there's record of it somewhere at the church."

She closed her eyes on a long sigh. "It was a long time ago, Hazel."

Sandra met her gaze again. "You cannot tell *anyone* what I'm about to say. Please."

Hazel nodded. "Of course."

"Robert was off in New York City helping with a senator's campaign. I was young and all alone, so I sought comfort from the one place I trusted. The church."

Hazel braced herself, knowing this story would not be good.

"Father Christopher was a new priest to our town. You wouldn't know it now, but he was handsome back then. And understanding. So understanding. I didn't plan for anything to happen. One day, I was in the chapel praying for strength, and he joined me on a pew. Next thing I knew, we were kissing, and, well, I'm not proud of what happened after that."

Hazel wanted to ask if Father Christopher had encouraged her to commit adultery right there in the chapel, but she'd probably be best to let that go. "He took advantage of your loneliness."

Mrs. Elwood nodded. "I didn't realize it back then. I just thought he was new to town and lonely, too."

"But priests are in a position of power, and what he did was wrong."

"Oh, trust me. I figured that out quickly, but by then, it was too late. He said he'd fallen in love with me, that he'd leave the church if I'd leave my husband, and we could be together. Of course, that would never happen."

"And he was okay with your decision?"

"He wasn't happy, but what could he do? It was his job to counsel me to work on my marriage, and even though he didn't, if he would have said anything to anyone, it would have cost him his career. He could have tried to ruin my marriage, but quite frankly, Robert needed the money and prestige my family carried, so he never would have left me."

Oh, the sordid affairs. "Did the mayor ever find out?"

Mrs. Elwood shook her head. "I don't think so. If he did, he never mentioned anything. Up until today, I thought I'd left that all behind me."

Hazel snorted. "Funny how life never seems to let that happen."

"So true." Mrs. Elwood focused a hard gaze on Hazel. "Why are you telling me this? Why now?"

She had to be honest with the poor woman who might have her life implode on her, too. "Some see you as a suspect in Father Christopher's murder. Your husband is running for office, and you, or he, might be desperate enough to keep this information hidden."

She released a long sigh. "Well, I guess I can see that point. Although, I'd had no idea he'd made a written record of our interactions all those years ago. We never spoke of it again. Why would I worry it would come back now?"

Hazel shrugged. "I don't know. Doesn't seem that you would, and it doesn't seem that the mayor had a clue and, therefore, no motive to kill."

Mrs. Elwood lifted her brows. "Do the police know?" Her expression dropped. "Oh, Lord. That's why Officer Bartles was following us, right? He's watching our actions."

She couldn't outright confess what Peter had told her. "I think that makes a lot of sense."

Sandra nodded sadly. "I do, too. I also think I should get to the police station as soon as possible before this gets further out of hand. Thank you, Hazel, for this information. It's certainly not what I wanted to hear, but I can work on solving issues now."

Hazel nodded and shook the woman's proffered hand. As Mrs. Elwood walked away, Hazel realized her husband wasn't the only one with smooth political moves.

CHAPTER TWENTY

Hazel watched Peter tighten the screw on the last turquoise bistro chair she'd purchased for outside her teashop. For an hour, she'd watched him work. She'd appreciated her personal brand of eye candy while she'd filled him in on her conversation with the mayor's wife.

Peter dropped the wrench into his toolbox and chuckled. "Yeah, I'd thought Bartles would have a cow when the mayor marched him into my office and told me what had happened."

That would have been the best show ever. "I wish I could have spied on them."

He grinned as he stood. "It was pretty glorious. I let Mayor Elwood rake him over the coals a few times before I told him I'd handle the situation. The mayor left in a huff, and for a minute, I thought John might cry."

"Seriously? That shouldn't make me happy, but it does. Just a little."

"Same. I would say he learned a good lesson on how to hone his etiquette when dealing with others."

She snickered and eyed the two bistro sets. "Thanks so much for your help. They look really great." Especially with the bright lime green awning she'd had placed last week.

She'd hoped the display said, "Come sit in my shade and enjoy something cool and refreshing", and that customers would want one of the new iced teas she'd begun selling in her shop. Tastes were still free, but she'd hoped potential customers would be so tempted that they'd want a big glass of tea instead.

Peter scooted the last chair into place beneath the table, and then stepped back to join her for a look. "Fantastic, if I do say so myself."

She grinned and placed a sweet kiss on his cheek. "I say so, too. I'm going to put pots of purple petunias and orange marigolds on each of them. Even if no one ever pauses long enough to sit, the added beauty should encourage shoppers to at least slow down and notice my shop."

He cast a sideways glance at her. "Are you having difficulty with sales?"

She placed her hands on her hips in a sassy gesture. "Not even. I'll have you know, I'm having my website redesigned as we speak so I can start selling the newest blends online to accommodate out-of-town customers who've requested it."

His eyes shone with pride. "That's really great. I'm proud of you."

"Thank you."

The sound of a loud, rumbling engine caught her attention, and she glanced up the street to see Victor and his ridiculously hot, but stupid Harley coming down the road. "Ugh." She shifted her gaze to Peter hoping he wouldn't notice.

But, of course, he had. Everyone looked when a powerful engine motored by.

Peter caught her gaze and smiled. "Boyfriend, huh?"

She rolled her eyes and turned her back to the road. "I don't know who you're talking about because *you're* my boyfriend. In fact, boyfriend, there's something else you can help me with inside."

She took his hand and tugged him toward the door of her shop.

He opened the door, and she stepped in. Victor drove by just as Peter followed. Before the door could shut behind them, Peter launched forward, bumping into her before he caught himself.

She gasped in surprise, and he grunted. He glanced back at the floor as though to see what had tripped him.

Hazel clenched her jaw knowing very well what had happened. A juvenile trick she'd learned in high school. If she could hex Victor from where she stood, she would.

"I think the threshold on your doorframe is a little high."

She widened her eyes in concern. "That's not good. I'll have someone look at it right away. I certainly don't need any of my older customers tripping and falling."

He nodded. "Good idea."

And by having someone look at it, she meant she'd be scanning those darned spell books for anything that might protect Peter from future attacks.

Peter glanced at his watch. "I need to get back to work before too long. You said there was something in here you needed help with?"

A teasing grin tickled her mouth. "Why, yes, there is, Chief Parrish. My lips have been feeling a tad neglected lately, and I thought perhaps you could pick up the slack."

A sexy chuckle rumbled from his chest. "You've called the right man to help." He pulled her hard against him, and she loved the way her body collided with his.

"Yes, I did," she said with a laugh. "You're the best kisser I know. Though, unfortunately, I won't be able to recommend you to anyone."

"That's okay. I'm a one-woman man." He lowered his mouth to hers and devoured her with a fiery kiss.

When he pulled away, she released a breathless sigh. "Perfect. Now my day is complete."

"Mine, too." He grinned. "What are you doing the rest of today?"

"I'll be here alone most of the time. Gretta is taking her grandmother to a doctor's appointment in Salem. Cora is supposed to stop by in a while."

Hazel had ancestry searching left to do on her family tree before her line reached Clarabelle's level. Unfortunately, Sarah's family line had mirrored hers up until that point. If she was about to discover Sarah was also related to Clarabelle, she couldn't do it alone.

Not if the outcome was as she feared.

"Sounds fun," Peter said. "Are you going to be home later tonight?"

"Yes, I'll be hanging out with Mr. Kitty." She wasn't sure she'd be in any shape for company, but she knew he was fishing for an invite. If he flat out asked, she'd agree. Otherwise, she'd pretend that subtle hint had slipped right past her.

He kissed her once more. "Care if I stop by?"

"Not at all," she lied. "You know I love to see you."

She inhaled a slow breath and reminded herself not to fret over chickens before she had eggs.

"Hey," he said, his expression brightening. "Before I leave, I wanted to tell you that you were correct. We've found Karen's mother and confirmed Karen was Father Christopher's daughter. Still can't find any correlation between the two deaths, though. Karen's mother had already heard about the May Day Curse and preferred to believe that was what had taken her daughter and not a case of vindictive homicide–slash–suicide."

There had to be something they were missing. "Keep working on it. You might find something. I've been thinking of trying to find a way to get to know Dan Cullpepper and see what I can get him to tell me."

Peter leaned back and stared down at her with an offended look. "Don't you think I've tried?"

She teasingly traced a finger across his bottom lip and smiled. "Sometimes, I discover much more than you or your officers do, dear chief."

He shook his head in a playful warning. "Uh-huh. But really, don't bother. He and his wife were both out of town, confirmed alibis."

She blew a frustrated breath upward, stirring her hair. "I feel like we're getting nowhere. If it's not Dan, the mayor or his wife, then who? Lucy or Rosalinda? I don't want to believe it's either one of them."

"Yeah. The district attorney is pushing for us to arrest Lobster Lucy, but I don't think we have enough evidence. If her motive was recent, I'd be more inclined, but if she really wanted to punish Father Christopher for his bad guidance, I think she would have done it before now."

Hazel nodded thoughtfully. "Rosalinda has motive, too, but not a strong one, and hers is old. Though I still feel like she's hiding something more."

He released a frustrated breath. "I tried to get her to open up to me the other day about what she had in her files about the mayor and his wife, but her lips were shut as tight as an oyster with a prized pearl."

She chuckled at his comparison. "Thank you for not outing me to her."

"If I could use it in court, I would have."

She narrowed her gaze, searching the energy to see if he was serious. "No, you wouldn't."

He gave her a sly smile. "I might, so you'd better mind your own business and stay out of trouble."

She met his smile with one of her own. "I promise to try harder to be good."

Then they both laughed.

Peter gestured toward the outside of her shop with a tip of his head. "Looks like Cora is here. Bonus for you, Lucy is with her."

Hazel caught them surveying her new outdoor furniture and grinned. Lucy's timely arrival would give her another chance to question her without being obvious, and it would also put off the research she intended to complete with Cora's support.

Peter slid his hands up both side of her cheeks and placed a possessive kiss on her lips. "Don't forget you promised to behave."

She gave him her most innocent smile. "Of course."

Though if the opportunity presented itself for her to learn more about Lucy, she couldn't be blamed.

The chief left her shop, calling out a "hey, ladies" as he passed Cora and Lucy. They responded with friendly hellos and Hazel joined them outside.

"Cora, Lucy," Hazel said. "So good to see you both. Why don't you be the first to try my new bistro sets, and I'll grab us some iced teas."

"I'm down," Lucy said and lowered herself into one of Hazel's adorable chairs.

Cora dragged a chair from the other table and sat in it, leaving an empty place for Hazel.

She hurried inside, filled clear plastic cups with ice and poured recently-brewed Pineberry Bush tea over them. She added lids and straws, and carried the pretty red drinks outside where hopefully others would see them and want their own.

She placed a cup in front of each of them on the table and took her seat. "Thanks for helping me advertise today."

Lucy glanced at the glasses, their surroundings, and nodded. "Yeah, who wouldn't want some of this?"

"It's perfect, Hazel," Cora added. "I might consider adding a few outdoor tables, too. Though I'm not sure how the servers would feel about having to monitor double areas. Let me know how yours works, okay?"

Hazel sipped her iced tea, still loving the new combination, and nodded. "Of course."

She should probably keep up with the niceties for a few more minutes, but she couldn't wait any longer to share her news. She leaned closer to the center of the table. "Did you guys know that Karen Bernard was Father Christopher's daughter?"

Cora spouted a stunned "no", but Lucy seemed unaffected.

Hazel focused her gaze on Lucy. "You don't seem surprised."

Lucy remained stoic for a moment and then nodded. "I knew. I became friends with Karen a few years back, not long after she moved to town. She didn't tell me about her father for a long time, and when she did, she asked me to keep quiet."

"So, she knew the Father was her father." One less coincidence to contend with.

"Yeah, she knew. She moved here because she wanted to know more about the man who'd deserted her mother before she was ever born."

Cora's features turned disappointed. "He just up and left? What kind of man does that?"

"The Father Christopher kind," Lucy said matter-of-factly. "He was almost done with priest school, or whatever you call it. If the church knew he had an illegitimate child, they would have kicked him to the curb. He'd told her mother he'd send support money and that he'd come back for her after he'd been established. He said he could pretend to fall in love with the poor woman and her child, and no one would suspect. But the jerk took off and never looked back."

Hazel sat back against her chair, flabbergasted. "That's incredible." She wished she could add to the story and tell them what he'd done to Mrs. Elwood, but she couldn't cause the woman more pain or angst.

Cora set her cup on the table. "Did Karen ever confront him?"

Lucy shook her head. "No. After she discovered who he was and what he was, she had no desire to become his known kin. I'm not sure why she stuck around town after that."

The gears in Hazel's brain cranked up to full speed. "Would she have wanted her father dead? Could she have poisoned the strawberry tart before she'd had the accident and died?"

Lucy nodded. "Maybe. I mean, she knew I was baking him a special tart, so yeah, I think she could have had a chance. Whether she did or not, we'll never know."

Hazel wondered at her quick response, but then again, having the blame cast on someone else would be a great thing in her shoes, and Karen could no longer be punished. Though if it wasn't Karen, Lucy might be helping a killer go free.

Hazel couldn't say she wouldn't do the same in her situation. Life in prison for murder carried a hefty sentence. Such a conundrum.

Cora shook her head. "I don't know. I didn't see her there that day, and I'm not sure I ever saw her enter the church at all. She'd be a sore thumb if she did, wouldn't she?"

Lucy shrugged. "Can't say. I'm just saying it's possible. The hate the woman carried for the man was powerful."

Hazel couldn't say she hated her father for deserting her, but then again, she'd had a great childhood with her mother and aunts around. If circumstances were different, then maybe.

Lucy cleared her throat and stood. "Look, I gotta go, ladies. Promised I'd help Rosalinda at the church, and I'm already late. Thanks for the walk, Cora, and the tea, Hazel. I appreciate having friends like you."

Hazel smiled. "Of course."

Cora stood and hugged her. "You're the one who's the amazing friend. I'd be in trouble without you."

Lucy gave them both a warm grin and then turned away with a wave. "Catch you on the flipside."

Hazel and Cora remained silent for several moments until Lucy was halfway down the block. Then Hazel sighed. "I feel so bad for her."

Cora nodded. "You can see in the way she walks that she's carrying the weight of the world on her shoulders. I think she's hopeful that she will be exonerated, especially since they haven't arrested her yet, but it has to be a huge worry."

"I can't even imagine." Hazel took a long sip from her drink, and then reset her emotions as best she could.

She'd asked Cora to stop by for a very important reason, and she supposed it was time to reveal that beast and slay it. "How about we take these drinks inside? I can only take so much heat during the day."

"Same," Cora said and stood. "I think being inside all the time has made me intolerable of the sun and heat."

Hazel stood and held the door open for her friend. As she followed her inside, she sent a silent prayer to the Blessed Mother hoping the next few minutes ended with insight and happiness.

CHAPTER TWENTY-ONE

Hazel led the way into the backroom where she had her laptop open to the ancestry page. She pulled two stools to that area so that they could sit. "Thanks for making time for me today."

Cora glanced at the screen with an interested but uncertain look and then back to Hazel. "You were a little cryptic, but of course I came. I'll always be here for you."

Cora's declaration sent Hazel's emotions swimming for the surface.

"Hey," Cora said and wrapped an arm around her shoulders. "Tell me what's wrong."

Hazel inhaled a shaky but fortifying breath. "I've been doing some research on my ancestry and discovered a few things that could have a significant impact on my life. And I'm really scared."

Cora turned to the screen again. "Like what?"

"Like..." She forced another breath. "Like I think I'm related to Peter's dead wife. I think she's part of Clarabelle's lineage."

Her eyes popped wide. "Sarah was? Show me."

It took them several minutes to search through other possibilities, but when they finished, the answer stared them both in the face screaming disaster.

Cora slumped in her chair. "Oh..."

The tone of her friend's voice magnified by five hundred was exactly how she felt. "This will break us," she whispered.

Cora drew her brows together. "You and Peter? No. Why would it?"

She snorted in disbelief. "Because his wife's death is the reason I'm now in Stonebridge."

"Yeah." Cora obviously wasn't buying into it. "But you didn't kill her. Or even cause her to be killed. That's on someone else."

"Yeah," Hazel countered. "But I'm the by-product of that disaster. Once Peter knows, he'll think of that every time he sees me. How can he not be resentful of me over time? What if he secretly wishes Sarah was still here and not me?"

Her voice broke on the last words. She wrapped her arms tight around her midsection as though that might protect her heart.

The expression on Cora's face seemed uncertain, too. "I don't know, Hazel, but I think you've got to trust him with this one. It's your only option."

"I could leave. I could pack up what I own and head back to Boston, or to someplace he could never find me."

Cora looked at her like she was crazy. "And you think that will solve everything?"

"He won't have to see my face everywhere he goes."

"You're talking about breaking the man's heart. A man who's already been through hell. How could you even consider it?"

She cupped her hand over her mouth. "I'm a horrible person," she said with muffled words.

"No." Cora removed her hand and pressed it between her own. "You're a wonderful, compassionate person who has a relationship with a kind and caring man. Trust yourself and more importantly, trust him."

"I'm not sure I can."

Cora's gaze turned stern. "Of course, you can."

She exhaled, but it didn't relieve the pressure on her heart. "He's coming to my house tonight."

Her friend gave her a firm nod. "Then it looks like you have your opportunity to tell him. Don't sit on this, Hazel. It will only fester and hurt you both more in the long run. Be honest with the man, and then give him some space if he needs it to process. Trust me. He's not going anywhere."

Hazel prayed her friend was right. If she'd thought she'd done hard things in life before, they were nothing compared to this.

The rest of the day dragged by excruciatingly slow. Every second was consumed with imagining the look on his face, the angst that would pour from him and eat her soul.

By the time she walked through her door, she could barely hold together her frayed emotions. She brought her laptop to the couch and pulled up the website again. With painstaking precision, she traced her lineage to Clarabelle and then followed the line back down to where it split off from Sarah's. They were practically cousins.

She was dating the husband of her dead cousin.

A wave of nausea rolled through her, and she questioned the universe's sanity. Was this the Karma bus coming for her for some misdeed she couldn't remember?

She closed the laptop and set it on the coffee table before collapsing back onto the couch pillows. She played out different scenarios of how this might end after she'd told Peter, and none of them were good.

He'd never be able to look at her again without thinking of his dead wife.

When the doorbell rang, she didn't move. Mr. Kitty climbed out from beneath the coffee table where he'd been watching her. When the doorbell rang a second time, he meowed, impatient that she wasn't getting up.

She should. She needed to, but her body wouldn't respond.

Loud knocks on the door jolted her like punches. The hinges on her front door squeaked, and she turned in shock. She was certain she'd locked it. But there was Peter striding toward her with deep concern etched on his face. *"Hazel."*

Mr. Kitty trotted along behind him, and she knew he was the one who'd unlocked the door for Peter.

Traitor.

Peter dropped to his knees on the carpet before the couch. "What's happened? Why didn't you answer the door?"

She tried to speak, but only muffled sobs escaped. In the next few moments, she'd change his life, and not for the better. She hated herself to the core for that.

He cupped her face and moved in close to her, so she couldn't focus on anything else. "Are you hurt?"

She placed a hand over her heart and then slowly did the same to him.

"Your heart hurts? My heart hurts? Jesus, Hazel, talk to me."

She closed her eyes for a long moment, searching for a shred of strength. Soft fur rubbed against her arm, and she opened her eyes to find Mr. Kitty squirming his way next to her on the couch.

He was there for her. He'd give her strength. She wasn't in this alone.

Knowing that brought more tears to her eyes, and she worked to blink them away. She cleared her throat and managed a partial sitting position. "I learned some really bad news today. And it's...it's going to hurt both of us."

His features darkened, and she sensed the shield he'd try to use to block the pain. "Tell me, Hazel. Tell me now."

Her breath shook her lungs as she inhaled, and she was grateful she had the couch beneath her for support. "Remember how I explained to you about the curse that would ensure someone from each of the original witches' families would always live in Stonebridge? Even if she didn't know she was a witch?"

He narrowed his gaze and nodded.

"I've discovered who I replaced."

He held her gaze for several long moments, and then his expression crumbled. Anguish ripped across his features, and he shook his head. "No."

She nodded. "I was drawn here because Sarah died."

Another sob escaped her, and Mr. Kitty meowed in response. He stood and rubbed against her arm until she placed a hand on his soft fur.

"She wasn't a witch," Peter whispered.

Hazel nodded. "I don't know whether she knew or not, but she was."

Warmth and comfort from her cat filled her. It wasn't enough to chase away the sorrow, but his presence did take the edge off.

She was certain Mr. Kitty was using his power to absorb it, and gratitude gently rocked her soul. "I'm so sorry, Peter. I would change it if I could."

He wiped the moisture from his eyes and stood. She feared he'd turn and walk away. Instead, he lifted her shoulders and slipped behind her, cradling her back against his chest, and holding her with a fierce embrace.

She wrapped her arms over his and searched for his fingers. Mr. Kitty climbed onto her stomach, lying on top of their clasped hands.

Hazel wasn't sure how long they stayed that way. Peter's chest stopped shaking from his controlled, quiet crying, and her tears eventually dried up, too, leaving her drained of emotion.

"Will you stay with me tonight, Peter?" she whispered. "I don't mean sex, but I won't sleep unless I know you're okay, and I really don't want to be alone right now."

"Yeah," he said in a low, gravelly voice next to her ear. "I don't want to be alone, either."

They made their way toward her bedroom. After Hazel had changed into a t-shirt and pair of flannel shorts, she climbed into bed next to Peter. He'd discarded his pants but kept his t-shirt on.

She slid next to him, allowing him to cradle her against his chest. The rhythmic thumping of his heart brought her comfort, and she slipped a hand across his chest until her fingers curved over his shoulder.

Beyond exhausted, she allowed sleep to chase away her pain and angst. She didn't know what tomorrow would bring, but she still had Peter in her life, and that was all she could ask for.

CHAPTER TWENTY-TWO

Hazel woke the next morning to the scents of bacon and coffee. She glanced to the empty space in her bed, sad to find he'd woken without her. But, with things being so tentative right now, she could understand.

She padded into the kitchen and managed to smile when she caught Peter feeding small pieces of bacon to Mr. Kitty. "Bribery, is it?"

He lifted his gaze, and she soaked up the warmth she found there. His features still looked ragged from the night before, but his aura was clear. "I think we're buddies."

Mr. Kitty meowed, and Peter tossed him another bit.

She scoffed. "I've fed him for days. Weeks. And he doesn't love me like that."

A kind smile turned Peter's features. "I'm pretty sure he loved both of us a lot last night."

Emotion welled, but she forced it down. If Peter could hold it together, so could she. "Yeah. You're right. I guess when I really need him, he's there."

Mr. Kitty rubbed against Peter's jean-clad legs and then snatched the rest of the bacon from his hand and ran. She and Peter both laughed.

He stood, and she walked into his open arms. "He might love us," she said. "But he's not going to let us think we're the boss."

Peter shrugged. "That's okay."

Hazel hugged him as tight as she could, once again taking solace from the strong beat of his heart. She leaned back and glanced up. "Are you okay?"

He nodded. "I think so. Learning that about you and Sarah was quite a shock, but I've thought about it. I can think you've stolen her place, or that you're the gift to help me heal and love again."

Blessed Mother, she loved his resiliency. It truly was a gift. "I hope I can be that person who helps you heal and find love again."

He squeezed her tight. "You already are."

She closed her eyes and held him for several long moments, absorbing the love that flowed from him and then, in return, sending her love to him.

"Hungry?" he finally asked.

She pulled away. "I think so, surprisingly."

"I hope that you don't mind that I made coffee instead of tea."

She snorted. "You do realize that the coffee you made and the coffeemaker you used are mine, right? Like it's not a sin to drink something other than my teas."

He grinned. "Point taken."

Together, they whipped up scrambled eggs and toast, and then sat together at the table to eat. Hazel loved how easy it was to be with him, and how much he filled that once-hollow spot inside her.

Peter lifted a piece of toast dripping with butter. "I've been thinking about the case."

Her brows shot up. "Are you serious?"

She would have thought he would have been mulling over their situation like she had been, but he seemed to have accepted things and moved on.

He gave her a sarcastic smile. "It beats the alternative."

She had to give him that. "Okay. What have you been thinking?"

"I think you're right. Odds are stacking against Rosalinda."

She was surprised to find he'd picked her. "What's convinced you that it's her?"

"She's the only one who still seems to be very angry at Father Christopher. You know that list you found?"

She nodded.

"I've been thinking. What if it was a list of people she could use to take the spotlight off her? Other more obvious suspects? She knows the church grounds well. She could have slipped in through a side door, especially if she still had keys to the building. With all the commotion out front with the cook-off, no one would notice. She mentioned to me that she knew in advance about Lucy's strawberry tart, so…"

Hazel considered his points and nodded thoughtfully. "You might be right. Lucy as a suspect has bothered me all along. I mean who would poison her own tart? As soon as the cause of his death was discovered, the evidence would point right to her. That would be a crazy move."

Peter pointed a determined fork at her. "Exactly."

"So, how are you going to prove it?"

He grinned. "I thought you could do that for me, Miss Smartypants."

She relaxed another notch, so grateful things between them were good again. "If I keep solving all your cases for you, you're going to have to start paying me your salary."

"Oh, you think you're that good, do you?"

She beamed. "As a matter of fact."

"Your advice then, Chief Hardy," he teased.

"Bring her in for questioning again. Go a little harder on her this time. She doesn't seem that strong-willed."

His grin grew bigger. "Hardline tactics, huh?"

"Why not? Maybe you should sic Officer Bartles on her."

They both laughed, and all seemed right in her world again.

"Or maybe..." She lifted a finger and pointed it at her temple. "We should look at Rosalinda's ancestry, too. Maybe there's a connection there. I've been on a roll lately, so why not?"

He shrugged. "Why not?"

Hazel retrieved her laptop and took some time first to show him how Sarah's and her own paths intersected and continue back to Clarabelle.

Sadness haunted his features, but he gave her a smile anyway. "Maybe that's why I originally said you reminded me of her."

"Maybe so."

She reset the search history and typed in Rosalinda Valentine. Married, but her husband had died ten years ago. No children listed.

Peter touched the screen. "Click there on her mother and siblings."

The program revealed her mother had been dead for twenty-two years. She had two sisters, both younger than her and both married.

Peter snorted. "Well, I'll be a dead goat's daddy."

His comment ripped her from investigation mode. "You'll be a *what*?"

"A dead goat's daddy." He shrugged. "It's just a saying, Hazel. Don't worry about it."

Okay... She gave a sarcastic blink and returned her focus to the computer.

Peter tapped the screen again. "Rosalinda's sister is Lisa Bernard."

Pieces clicked, and she turned to him in surprise. "I'll be a dead goat's daddy if that's not Karen Bernard's mother."

"See? You're getting the hang of it." He chuckled. "But seriously, yes. That's her mother's name. If we're correct, and I think we are, Rosalinda is the sister of the woman Father Christopher deserted."

"And Karen Bernard's aunt. Wow."

Peter scooted his chair back from the table. "I need to bring her into the station and have another chat."

Hazel lifted hopeful brows. "Can I come?"

"You can't be in the interrogation room, Hazel. You know that."

She pouted, and he rolled his eyes.

"Fine. You can come with, but you'll have to wait in my office."

She jumped up. "Deal."

CHAPTER TWENTY-THREE

Hazel waited in Peter's patrol car while he ran inside his house to change into a uniform. Then, because it was during business hours, they headed straight to the church where Rosalinda would likely be instead of her home.

Peter pulled alongside the road in front of the historical church and parked behind a black Harley. "Looks like your boyfriend is here."

She closed her eyes on a long sigh and shook her head. "Why..."

He jerked open his door and stepped out. "Who cares?"

He grinned at her through the front windshield as he walked to her side.

She pondered that for a moment and realized he was right. Who cares?

Victor was no longer part of her life, and he could only be again if she gave him space in her thoughts. She was so over that.

She linked hands with Peter as they approached the front door and opened her senses. If Victor was close by, she'd rather know where he was so that she wouldn't be blindsided when he appeared.

They found him painting the trim in the hallways near Rosalinda's office. Even with paint spattered over his clothes and his forearms, he still looked good.

He stared at Peter for a long moment with a dull expression. Then he turned his gaze to her and smiled. "Hello, goddess."

Peter's fingers tightened around hers, and she yanked in her flailing reserve. She would not let Victor affect her.

Victor's gaze slid to Peter again and made her nervous. If he tried another stunt...

Peter stepped closer to Victor and forced him to lift his gaze higher. "It doesn't look like Rosalinda is in her office. Do you know where she is?"

Victor set the paintbrush on a tray and stood. He and Peter were roughly the same height, both dark-haired, both built. One had a heart of gold. The other...she wasn't sure Victor even had a heart.

Instead of answering Peter, Victor stared, his gaze challenging Peter's abilities.

She could practically taste the thick testosterone pulsing in the air. "Do you know where she is, Victor?"

He blinked and shifted his gaze to her. "Not sure. She left with Lucy a couple of minutes ago. Rosalinda seemed scared, and Lucy was agitated as—"

"Thank you, Victor." She didn't need him to expound any more than that.

Peter lifted his chin. "What did Lucy do to make you think she was agitated?"

Hazel, too, was already reworking her theory about the case. If Lucy was angry and Rosalinda scared, that didn't bode well for Lucy.

Victor turned to Hazel. "Is he still talking to me?"

Her frustration exploded. "Can you just answer the question?"

He tilted his head to a downward angle and stared at Peter with cold eyes. "They didn't need to do anything for me to know. I have that ability."

Recognition dawned in Peter's eyes, and he glanced at Hazel in question.

She wasn't going to answer. Not here. Not now. "Is there anything else you can tell us, Victor?"

He released a long-suffering sigh. "Lucy demanded Rosalinda go with her to Gloucester. They were in a hurry. Didn't even notice me when they left."

Peter nodded. "Did you see a gun or other weapon?"

"No." The air around Victor tightened, and she feared he was about to let loose some magic.

She squeezed Peter's hand to draw his attention. "Let's go."

"Hey," Victor called after her, and she glanced back. "You're welcome for that information and for locking those cabinet drawers."

Her grateful smile came easily this time. "Thanks."

He gave a nod of acceptance.

She held tight to Peter's hand as they exited the building, monitoring him for any signs of malevolent activity caused by Victor.

She frowned at Peter when they were both back in the cruiser. "Gloucester? Why would she take Rosalinda there?"

Peter started the engine, put the vehicle in drive, and gunned the accelerator. "I don't know, but I'm going to see if I can catch up to them."

He snatched the two-way radio. "This is Police Chief Parrish. I need an APB for two females in a silver, late-model Buick Century. Lucy Flanigan and Rosalinda Valentine. They may possibly be heading toward Gloucester. One of them may be a hostage. Approach with care."

The male dispatcher repeated the chief's request to all units.

A few moments later, the dispatcher responded, saying an officer had noticed Lucy's silver sedan stopped at the gas station at the end of town only moments before.

Peter flipped on his lights and siren. "Got 'em."

He called in to have that unit follow but not engage the suspects. He'd be there momentarily.

Addictive excitement bubbled inside her as adrenaline flooded her veins. She'd always wondered what it would feel like to be in hot pursuit. "I know this is serious business, and someone's life might be in danger...but this is awesome."

Peter snorted and shook his head. "Some days it is awesome. But not today."

No, not today. "Do you think Lucy means to hurt her?"

He blew out a frustrated breath. "Lord, I hope not. Lucy does own an old rundown cabin where her ex used to go to get drunk and fish. It's possible they could be headed there."

"But why?"

He slowed to pass cars that had pulled to the side of the road and then sped up again. "That's the question."

A quarter mile past the gas station, she noticed a police cruiser ahead of them. "Look."

"I see them." He pressed harder on the accelerator.

The first unit slowed to let Peter pass and soon he was directly behind Lucy's car. Hazel shot a concerned glance toward Peter. "They aren't stopping."

"Don't worry. They won't get away."

He swung out around them, and Hazel shifted her gaze to the occupants in the other car. Lucy had her eyes glued to the road ahead while Rosalinda seemed to be yelling at her.

"Hang on," Peter said as he passed them and then cut to the lane in front of them. Slowly, he decreased his speed, and Hazel caught sight of the other police cruiser bringing up the rear with lights blazing.

When Peter had almost stopped, Lucy pulled off the side of the road causing her front bumper to dip down into the ditch.

Peter shoved the car into park and swung open his door. He unsnapped the strap holding his gun in place. "Stay here."

"Be careful," she whispered, but he'd already shut the door.

She released the seatbelt and turned to look over the seat toward the action. As he approached the car, her heart and brain agreed for once to note being in danger was a part of his life, and if she wanted him in hers, she'd have to accept it.

That didn't mean she couldn't layer him with a ton of protection spells before he walked out the door each morning. She wished she'd thought to give him Cora's medallion before he'd gotten out of the car.

Rosalinda's door opened, and she made a run for it. She scurried right past Hazel's window with low heels wobbling on the uneven ground and crazy eyes focused on the road ahead.

Hazel snorted in disbelief and tried not to laugh at the sad, but humorous sight. A few seconds later, an officer from the second car dashed after her. Hazel watched as he struggled to subdue her and finally had to force her to the ground.

With Lucy and Rosalinda both in custody, she shoved open her door and stepped out.

The defeated expression on Lucy's face broke her heart.

Peter frowned at Hazel, but she could see no reason to stay in the car. None of them seemed to be in immediate danger.

When Lucy caught sight of Hazel, she shook her head and dropped her gaze to the ground. Hazel hurried toward them.

"You shouldn't be here," Lucy said with a gruff voice. "You don't need to see this."

Rosalinda shook her head, anger pouring off her like lava from a volcano. "None of us should be here. Would be here, if not for your stupidity, Lucy."

Lucy shot a vengeful look toward her. "Shut up, Rosalinda. I was fine until you dredged up all that nasty business with Father

Christopher. I'd put my past behind me. Now look what you've done."

Peter took hold of Lucy's elbow. "Come on."

He guided her toward the back door of his car, opened it and helped her inside. The second officer, a new guy on Peter's team, ushered Rosalinda to the opposite side.

Hazel climbed in the car before Rosalinda had reached the passenger door.

She shifted to look toward the backseat. "What is she talking about, Lucy? What nasty business?"

Rosalinda scoffed as she was forced inside. "Don't say anything more, Lucy. You'll only make it worse."

"It's already worse, Rosalinda. They've figured us out. It's over."

Hazel tried to sense what stirred beneath the conversation, but too many emotions bounced all over the place like ping pong balls. "Tell me you didn't kill Father Christopher, Lucy."

Lucy stared, her once bright aura now nearly black. "I've done some bad things, Hazel. We both have."

Peter entered the car as Lucy finished her sentence. He shoved his keys into the ignition and started the cruiser. "I'll remind you both. You've been read your Miranda rights. Anything you say can and will be used against you in court."

"See," Rosalinda hissed.

Lucy folded her arms across her large chest. "Shut up, Rosalinda."

Hazel straightened in her seat and glanced toward Peter. She wished he'd let them keep talking, but she could understand that he'd been trying to give them the best chance at what the future would bring.

But she had questions. So many questions.

EPILOGUE

Hazel waited on a bench outside the charming building that housed the police station, enjoying the pinks and oranges of dusk painted across the sky as the sun said goodnight. A cool breeze teased her senses, dancing through her curls and bringing the lush scent of freshly mowed grass to her. An owl hooted in greeting, and she scanned her surroundings looking for it.

She'd always loved this time of night, when the bright world began to settle, and the mysteries would peek out from the shadows.

She'd ended up working most of the day while Peter was privy to all the details about the case that she was dying to know. He'd finally messaged her not long ago, asking if she wanted to meet for an evening stroll.

Of course, the answer was yes.

At the sound of footsteps behind her, she turned and watched as the man who'd stolen her heart stepped from the building.

"Hey, beautiful," he said in a low voice.

"Hey, handsome," she returned.

She stood when he reached her. "Long day. Did you get everything sorted?"

He released a weighted sigh and slipped his fingers through hers. "Some. I'm sure not all though. These people have created a spider web of their lives. All are trapped, and none will be the same afterward."

He directed them across the street toward the nearest park. She'd never strolled through it after dark and found she loved its shadow side.

Still, her heart was heavy with the day's events. "Does this mean Lucy did kill Father Christopher?"

"Yeah," he answered with his voice full of sadness. "But Rosalinda helped."

"Both of them? I mean I could tell from what Rosalinda said in the car that she wasn't completely innocent, but I thought maybe she was covering for Lucy."

"Nope. Lucy made the tart, but Rosalinda was the mastermind behind it. She played on Lucy's pain, ripping open old scars and rubbing past thorns in deep."

He tugged her off the path toward a bench that overlooked the stream. At night, she couldn't see much of the water, but the cheerful gurgling sounds seemed more prominent. "Let's sit and breathe some of this fresh air."

She sat next to him on the bench, and he wrapped his arm around her.

After watching him in action that day, she appreciated his strength more than ever. "I'm guessing Rosalinda was motivated by what Father Christopher had done to her sister."

He nodded. "From what Rosalinda told us, her sister Lisa was a beautiful girl excited to attend college. She'd met Father Christopher, before he was a priest, while she was working at a fast food place near both of their schools. He'd charmed her and then gotten her pregnant. Sadly, her parents kicked her out, leaving Rosalinda's sister to fend for herself and her little one. Apparently, her sister has struggled ever since, often turning to drugs and alcohol."

"Not a good life for a child."

"Nope."

She wished she could curse him. "After all the bad things he did to others, I hope if there's a hell, he's rotting there."

"I'm sure he is." He stroked the back of her hand with his thumb. "Rosalinda was the one who finally tracked him down and moved here. Karen followed, hoping her mother had lied about him. When she discovered she hadn't, her life basically went downhill as well."

Sad how one person could destroy so many. "Lucy was a friend to Karen, though."

"Which was Lucy's downfall. If not for that, Rosalinda wouldn't have been able to drag her back in. But her heart broke for poor Karen, and after what Father Christopher had put Lucy through during her marriage, I guess it was enough to send her over the edge."

That broke Hazel's heart more than anything. "Do you think the courts will show her leniency because of Rosalinda's manipulations?"

He hugged her tighter against him. "I wish I could say yes, but that's not up to me. Let's hope so."

"Yes," she murmured. "Let's hope so."

They sat that way for a long time, both breathing in the cleansing night air.

"I'm glad my life isn't that convoluted."

He snorted. "You're not serious, right?"

"Of course, I'm serious. My life is good. I have you, my teashop, and an ornery old cat to love."

"You seem to be forgetting you're a witch in a town full of witch-haters."

She leaned her head against him. "I have hopes that may change one day."

"That would be nice."

She shifted to catch his gaze. "Hey, what about Karen? Did Lucy or Rosalinda give you any idea what made her crash that day? Suicide because she hated her life?"

"Nope. No clue. Both were certain she'd never do such a thing, and we found no suicide note. Mechanics couldn't find anything wrong with her car that might have caused her to lose control."

She sighed and leaned back against him. "Perhaps it's the May Day Curse after all."

He chuckled. "If you believe in that sort of thing."

Unfortunately, she was beginning to believe more and more. What could her ancestor have possibly done to punish the town all those years ago? She desperately wanted to find out. And fix it. Because Stonebridge spoke to her deep down, in her heart. It had become her home.

She glanced at the man by her side whose tapestry threads had intertwined so sweetly and securely with hers. And in that moment, following her heart, she felt as if she were capable of anything she desired. And what she desired was to live peaceably here, a good witch living among the townspeople in harmony. And to do that, she must locate the other witches to help undo the angry spells cast upon Stonebridge by her coven sisters three hundred years ago.

Peter squeezed her hand, and she turned to him, reminded of what the ancient spell books said: Better to follow your heart, or you're already dead.

A gentle breeze fluttered by, and she smiled back at him softly.

So mote it be.

****

If you enjoyed reading this book, the greatest gift you can give me is to tell a friend and leave a review at Amazon or Goodreads. It helps others find stories they might love and helps me to continue pursuing this crazy writing career.

Thank you and happy reading,
Cindy

Excerpt from THE FIFTH CURSE
Teas and Temptations
Cozy Mystery Series
Book Five

Hazel Hardy glanced over the sparkling crystal containers filled with various spiked and regular iced teas. She smoothed the pristine white linen tablecloth they rested on and gave the pink roses and baby's breath sitting in a nearby vase one last sniff.

Most of the people attending the wedding had already entered Stonebridge's oldest church, and it was time for her to as well. The ceremony would begin in ten minutes.

The sun drew closer to evening, and she hurried from beneath the billowy white tent where caterers would serve food during the reception. Her heels wobbled as she crossed the church lawn toward the large rough-hewn wooden doors that had been propped open for the celebration.

Cooler air, scented by the passing of centuries, greeted her as she entered. Cheerful voices echoed from the chapel, along with bounteous happy emotions.

Today was one of those good days in a person's life. She wished Peter could have abandoned his police chief duties and joined her.

As she entered the chapel, she gave an inward chuckle. Someone had finally tricked her into sitting on a church pew.

That was okay. She was glad to share the soon-to-be-wedded couple's happiness.

Hazel searched for Margaret, Peter's administrative assistant and one of her good friends, who had saved her a spot in the second to the last box of seats in the old church. Hazel opened the gate-like door to enter the enclosure and slipped onto the hard, wooden bench beside Margaret.

Her friend had chosen a champagne silk dress and matching hat with an enormous bow that was bigger than her head. Perfect attire if they'd been attending a royal wedding.

Margaret clutched a small purse with one gloved hand and lifted the other to whisper. "Good. You're here. They're almost ready to start."

Hazel smiled and nodded. "Just needed to make sure everything was perfect outside."

"I'm sure it is."

Hazel studied the guests and waited for the soft, melodic tune on the piano to switch to the Wedding March.

Five minutes passed.

Then ten.

Stress and nerves often slowed down ladies on the brink of marriage, but Hazel knew patience would reward the guests with a beautiful bride.

She'd been thrilled when Fiona Hoffstetter had contacted her. She hadn't known her personally, but Fiona's reputation as the best wedding planner in the area preceded her.

Fiona had told her that, although she no longer lived in town, she'd always loved the old church. Stonebridge was the most beautiful, quaint town she knew, and she and her fiancé had grown up in the area.

Fiona had said she'd heard fantastic things about Hazel's specialty teas and asked her to cater the drinks for her upcoming wedding. Coming from Fiona, a wedding planner herself, that was quite the compliment.

Hazel hadn't thought about branching out into catering, but maybe she should.

A snicker from behind them caught Hazel's attention, and she focused her senses in that direction.

"Can you imagine how much she's freaking out right now?" one woman said. "She's probably searching everywhere for her shoes."

Hazel narrowed her gaze, wondering if she'd misunderstood.

"Who's going to notice missing shoes?" another with a higher-pitched voice said. "Her veil is much more important."

Hazel opened her eyes wide and blinked. They'd stolen or hidden the bride's shoes and veil? She yearned to turn to see who could do such a cruel thing.

Margaret did exactly that. "Hush, Gwen. If you can't be nice, you shouldn't have come."

The pianist pounded out the first dramatic notes in the Wedding March, bringing their conversation to a halt. Hazel stood as the flower girl dressed in soft pink tulle scattered peach-colored rose petals down the aisle.

Hazel used the pretense of watching for the bride to enter the chapel as an excuse to turn toward the doors, giving her a perfect view of the women behind her.

She recognized Margaret's sister, Gwen, a voluptuous platinum blonde wearing a lime green dress with dramatic cleavage. She sat with two other twenty-something women. One with long black curls wore a fiery red dress, black gloves, and fantastic red shoes with three-inch heels. The other paled in comparison with light brown hair, dressed in baby blue, who also wore a hat, though not as elaborate as Margaret's.

In Hazel's mind, she couldn't conjure a good enough reason why Gwen and the other two would choose to play a joke on the bride. A woman's wedding day should be one of the most memorable in her life and already had enough anxiety to last for weeks.

Whispers in the crowd quieted as the veil-less bride stepped through the doors. Her flushed face carried obvious signs of stress, and she narrowed her gaze when she spotted the three women in the back row.

She knew.

As Fiona passed Hazel's pew, she stumbled. A quick snort of laughter escaped the woman in red, and her friends giggled in response. The bride's father placed a firm hand on Fiona's waist to steady her, and Hazel noticed her dress seemed a tad long.

Probably because of the lack of shoes.

Hazel caught sight of the nasty women's faces as they shifted to follow the bride's progress. They were all too focused on Fiona to notice Hazel's perusal. She wondered if Margaret was aware of their underhanded tactics.

Fiona's father kissed her cheek and handed her off to her beloved, a man named Arthur Wainswright.

"Wait until the itching starts," one of the women said, and they all three giggled.

Seconds after the words reached Hazel's ears, poor Fiona pretended to adjust the strap on her dress, but Hazel could see she'd used the action to cover her forearm rubbing across one of her breasts.

Hazel shook her head in complete disgust, wishing she could cast a small hex on the three women, so they would know what humiliation felt like.

Hazel suffered empathetically through the entire ceremony, feeling every inch of Fiona's discomfort and anxiety. When the priest announced them as husband and wife and Arthur leaned in for a kiss, Hazel turned, prepared to give the women a piece of her mind.

But they were gone.

Margaret huffed in disgust. "I cannot believe Gwen."

Hazel absorbed some of Margaret's embarrassment. "Sounds like the three of them played some nasty tricks on Fiona. Shoes? Veil? Something itchy?"

Margaret rolled her eyes. "I should have known Gwen wouldn't keep her promise to behave. Granted, she does have a right to be angry, but still."

That piqued her curiosity. "Why is she angry with Fiona?"

Her friend widened her eyes. "You haven't heard? Oh, my goodness. You're probably the only person in Stonebridge who hasn't."

Now, she really had her. "Tell me. You know I love a juicy story."

Margaret cast her gaze about them, but everyone seemed preoccupied on making their way to congratulate the newlyweds. "I shouldn't spread gossip since she's my sister, but if she's going to act this way, no one is going to forget anyway."

Hazel nodded in agreement.

"Fiona planned Gwen's wedding a few months back, before you arrived. Gwen had gained a few pounds between trying on her dress and the day of the wedding. When Gwen put on the dress, and it didn't fit, she panicked. I mean totally freaked out."

"I can only imagine."

"Well, Fiona stepped in to save the day and let out a seam. Gwen opted to not wear a bra to give her even more room."

Hazel sucked in a breath, fearing where this conversation might head.

Margaret must have caught the look on her face because she nodded. "Yep. That's right. They'd taken their vows. Gwen lifted her arms to place them around his neck for the kiss, and *rip*...." She screeched the last word.

As much as Hazel didn't approve of Gwen's behavior today, compassion for the poor woman flooded her. "Oh, no. How horrible."

"The guests got an eyeful, and Gwen ran to the dressing room and wouldn't come out for the whole reception. She believes Fiona should have known the thin threads of the remaining seam wouldn't hold, and she won't forgive her."

Hazel lifted her eyebrows and let them drop. What a mess. "Maybe she will now that she's gotten her revenge?"

Margaret snorted, the sound not matching her demure outfit. "Doubtful."

Her friend stood. "Enough of that. Let's go congratulate the couple."

You can find THE FIFTH CURSE, Teas and Temptations Cozy Mystery Series, Book Five, on Amazon.com.

Book List

TEAS & TEMPTATIONS COZY MYSTERIES (PG-Rated Fun):
Once Wicked
Twice Hexed
Three Times Charmed
Four Warned
The Fifth Curse
It's All Sixes
Spellbound Seven
Elemental Eight
Nefarious Nine

BLACKWATER CANYON RANCH (Western Sexy Romance):
Caleb
Oliver
Justin
Piper
Jesse

ASPEN SERIES (Small Town Sexy Romance):
Wounded (Prequel)
Relentless
Lawless
Cowboys and Angels
Come Back to Me
Surrender
Reckless
Tempted
Crazy One More Time

I'm With You
Breathless

PINECONE VALLEY (Small Town Sexy Romance):
Love Me Again
Love Me Always

RETRIBUTION NOVELS (Sexy Romantic Suspense):
Branded
Hunted
Banished
Hijacked
Betrayed

ARGENT SPRINGS (Small Town Sexy Romance):
Whispers
Secrets

OTHER TITLES:
Moonlight and Margaritas (Sexy Contemporary Romance)
Sweet Vengeance (Sexy Romantic Suspense)

About the Author

Award-winning author Cindy Stark lives with her family and a sweet Border Collie in a small town shadowed by the Rocky Mountains. She writes fun, witch cozy mysteries, emotional romantic suspense, and sexy contemporary romance. She loves to hear from readers!

Connect with her online at:
http://www.CindyStark.com
http://facebook.com/CindyStark19
https://www.goodreads.com/author/show/5895446.Cindy_Stark
https://www.amazon.com/Cindy-Stark/e/B008FT394W

Made in the USA
Monee, IL
14 April 2021